The Nine: Zane

by

Elle Arroyo

The Nine Series

The Nine: Zane

Contact Information: info@thewildrosepress.com

Cover Art by *Jennifer Greeff*

The Wild Rose Press, Inc.
PO Box 708
Adams Basin, NY 14410-0708
Visit us at www.thewildrosepress.com

Publishing History
First Edition, 2023
Trade Paperback ISBN978-1-5092-4664-9
Digital ISBN978-1-5092-4665-6

The Nine Series
Published in the United States of America

Dedication

To Neslie, for reading my first drafts and for the wine.

Chapter One

Zane

A ladybug darted out between the trees. A moose closing the distance behind it.

I rubbed my eyes to erase the imaginary image. I hadn't been on an acid trip since my early days in college. The rubbing didn't seem to work. The moose lunged onto the smaller, quicker ladybug as it tried to flank it to get to the small, dilapidated cabin twenty yards away. They both fell on the snow-covered ground and proceeded to wrestle.

"What did you put in my drink?" I asked Bennett, my driver, safety specialist, and good friend who obviously spiked my drink at some point during our six-hour flight into no-man's land somewhere in the ass crack of Maine.

"This is all kinds of wrong," Bennett said. "Should I shoot them both?"

Not an unusual thought coming from a trained assassin. I was packing too. In my line of work, one couldn't be too sure of anything. Though watching a ladybug attempting to throat punch a moose was a new one even for me.

The moose scampered to his feet just as the ladybug leapt onto his back, strangling it. The moose took heavy, careful steps toward the stairs of the cabin.

By this point, the moose's head had been turned at a severe angle, so it looked like it was staring at me with dead coal-colored eyes. The ladybug's antennae hung askew.

"Maybe we got the wrong place," I whispered, hoping we got the wrong place. The last thing I needed was to get between a moose and its ladybug who were back on the ground trying to smother each other. The ladybug managed to straddle the moose and was now fisting its antlers, banging its head on the snow-packed ground.

"This is the correct address," Bennett whispered, and wiped the condensation on the windshield in front of him to see better.

"Maybe we should come back some other time," I suggested.

"It took you five years to get here," Bennett reminded me. "You won't come back."

Bennett was right. I'd been pining for the man who had consumed my thoughts for the better part of five years. He'd been desperate and broken the one night we shared. Heartbroken by the woman he loved. I had intervened and shown him compassion. Something I'd never done before. He'd simply melted in my arms and left me needy. Needing to hold him. Needing to know he was okay. Needing to get a glimpse of how his life had turned out. Finally, Bennett called it and had me hire a private investigator where news surfaced that Eric Diaz had survived his divorce. As a successful writer, he jumped from state to state every few months, either seeking something or running. I sat on that information for eighteen months until the deal with my father had me flying to the edge of the world to seek what I truly craved.

Him.

To know once and for all if I had invaded his thoughts and soul, just like he invaded mine. To get him out of my system so I could move on.

Just then, the moose managed to extricate itself from the ladybug's hold and tore free from it. It sprinted up toward the cabin, momentarily losing traction on the slick ice and pin wheeling its arms just as the ladybug made a desperate attempt to flank it. Within reach, the ladybug had no chance. The moose grabbed the black dotted shell in a tight grip, using it as leverage before yanking the bug back a few steps.

"I bet you five bucks the ladybug wins," I said.

Bennett chuckled. "You're on."

The ladybug would not go quietly. In a last-ditch effort, it flung itself toward the moose's ankle and clung tight. The moose dragged the insane bug to the foot of the stairs then held onto the posts before pulling sharply away from the death grip. Once free, the moose sprinted up the steps, stumbled inside the cabin, and slammed the door on the ladybug, who was just pulling itself to its feet.

"Ha," Bennett said. "Pay up."

I slapped five bucks into his open palm and got out of the car.

The ladybug looked about ready to explode out of her shell. "Fine!" The small voice belonging to a woman who could've been twelve or thirty yelled out. Cute as a button. "Just so you know. You'll have to call Sheriff Swanky to come save you from that ridiculous costume, you, you, degenerate!" Then the ladybug broke out into a sinister laugh that drew chills up my spine that had nothing to do with the biting cold. Cute blew away in the wind with some of my sanity.

The ladybug stumbled back as the door to the cabin burst open and the moose stood in the doorway. I still couldn't figure out how the hell the person inside could see. The moose looked to be yelling at Bennett near the car.

"You, you, knacker!" a deep grumble said. At least that's what it sounded like. I didn't know what a knacker was, but it got ladybug to haul ass back through the woods without so much as a glance back.

I heard the door slam and the silence that followed was deafening.

I turned to Bennett for direction. He shrugged. *You're on your own, dude.* That shrug said.

I braved the wild and tried the door. It opened, and I stepped into the small cabin, closing the door behind me. The entire area included a small living room, kitchenette, and the loft bedroom above. The place was smaller than my closet in New York. I suddenly felt claustrophobic.

An angry growl led my attention to the moose, who had a pair of sharp shears against its throat. "Whoa," I said, lifting my hands. "Should I call Sheriff Swanky?"

"Hell no," the discombobulated voice said. I could tell it was a deep voice. A male voice. "I have to take this out. The zipper isn't working." He sounded on the verge of panic.

I approached the moose slowly. For some insane reason, the thought of the moose hurting itself sent a flair of dread into my gut. No, not a moose. A man. I was totally confused in more ways than I could fathom right now. The smart thing to do would be to run. Get back on that plane and go home. To hell with the shit that had been spiraling through me for years. I had learned to ignore worse things. I wasn't smart, though. "Let me do it for you."

"Who are you?" the moose asked, pointing the shears in my direction.

Had it been anyone else but this moose, I probably would've used my untraceable Ruger concealed in my holster and shot it in its freaky head. "Uh, I'm looking for Mr. Diaz. Eric Diaz?"

"That's me. Can you cut this off me?"

"Yeah." I approached slowly, just in case. I didn't trust many people, especially ones with weapons in their hands. I'd been shot, stabbed, clawed, and bitten way too many times to let down my guard. Even to a moose. I reached for the shears and the guy pulled back.

"How do I know you're not some sort of serial killer going to chop me up into little pieces?"

My stomach knotted. "What is it with you and serial killers?" He'd said the same thing to me five years ago.

The moose cocked its head, taking a moment to examine me. I suddenly felt nervous. A knee-jerk reaction, really. Something about the moose made me uneasy.

"Have we met?"

"I don't know. You don't look familiar."

"Ha. Ha. Everyone's a comedian," the moose said. I chuckled. I thought it was ridiculously hilarious. He handed me the shears and turned around, trusting me. I almost warned him that he probably shouldn't. "Just slice next to the zipper. I'd like to save the costume if I can."

I almost laughed at the insanity of it all.

After all this time, this scenario had not played out the way I'd expected. I wasn't even sure if it was the Eric I'd been craving since meeting him. "Don't move," I warned. He shivered under the costume. "I'm not going to hurt you. Just don't move." I waited until he stilled, then pinched the fabric and punctured a neat hole. I then carefully inserted one of the blades in the tear and sliced along the zipper. Once done, I stepped back and watched Eric peel out of the costume.

The moose had given him an extra foot height. Without it, Eric reached up to my chin. He had a thick head of dark curls and had thinned out since the last time I saw him. He shoved the costume down over his hips, down his legs, and stepped out of it, remaining in only a fitted tee-shirt that revealed his lean torso, boxer briefs that highlighted a nice ass, and long rainbow-colored socks that reached just under his knees. The guy looked so damn adorable I couldn't stop the smile that was plastered on my face.

It wasn't until he turned around, however, that I knew I'd regret following my gut with this one. He hadn't changed much, not that I had expected him to. His baby brown eyes were framed by thick, dark lashes. A scar just above his left brow left a bald spot I found endearing. He had a cleft on his nose, and thick, full lips I wanted to feel against my own. The temptation had me licking my lips. I'd hoped to get some sort of heated reaction from the guy. Some memory spark that would have him recognizing me. I got nothing but a curious look out of him.

I had to remember to breathe.

"Are you okay? You look like you're going to pass

out."

True. I felt dizzy. The space between us too narrow, the cabin walls too constricting. I needed air. It wasn't until he finally broke eye contact that I took a deep inhalation of breath and released it in a slow exhale.

I had always considered myself a good-looking man. I never had to work hard for what I needed in the bedroom, or the bathroom, kitchen, laundry room, or pool. Yeah, I had the all-American blond hair, blue eyes, ripped body that had both females and males looking my way. So to be forgotten by the one man I had incessantly thought of over the years left me deflated. Maybe hurt. Surely, disappointed. But definitely intrigued. I never, *ever*, backed out of what I wanted. And I had wanted this man for too damn long. I wasn't about to give up now that I finally found him. Not my style. I just had to play it to plan. Do not deviate and do not get distracted. Not even by his fine ass and thick full lips I would taste by the time my time in backcountry Maine came to an end.

Ladybug be damned. The moose was mine.

Chapter Two

Eric

The man in my kitchen looked so out of place. I had to take a moment to scrutinize the alienness of it all. First, the man looked like he crawled out of the cover of GQ. The expensive-looking suit he wore fit him perfectly. He stood over six feet, and had a tousle of blond hair with strands of lighter highlights. Accented with strong chiseled features and ocean blue eyes, the guy looked to be in his mid-twenties, at most. He definitely did not belong in my kitchen. And he was looking at me as if I were about to burst into confetti at any moment and he didn't want to miss it.

"What?" he finally asked under my scrutiny.

"You look ridiculous." Yeah, I had no filter. The reason my best friend had glued my costume shut so I'd suffocate to death.

"Says the man wearing a moose."

I flinched at the thought of wearing an actual moose. "Costume," I corrected him. "It's a moose *costume,* and I'll have you know moose are respected along these parts and, except for in Alaska, you'll find a healthy population of moose here. Have you ever seen one up close, Mr. Fancy Pants?" Yeah, I called him fancy pants. I was rambling. Something I did when a healthy dose of nerves rushed through me. Like now.

Although I wasn't sure why I was so nervous.

"It's Thomas," he said.

"Huh?" I lifted a brow.

"As opposed to Fancy Pants. My name is Thomas. And I can't say that I have ever seen a moose. Or a moose fighting a ladybug either until now, so thank you for that."

Unable to hold back my flush of embarrassment, I started to laugh. It took Thomas two seconds to join me. He had a nice laugh. It sounded as if he were clearing his pipes, never having laughed before. The glimmer in his blue eyes made them seem like two twinkling jewels.

"She looked really pissed, by the way," Thomas added on an inhale.

"She'll get over it," I admitted, wiping a stray happy tear.

"Should we report her to Sheriff Swanky?"

"Oh, God, no. Please. I don't think I can stand being pawed by that one again." I shivered at the thought of the sheriff declaring herself my savior for catching that runaway badger that had gone for my throat. Okay, I may have exaggerated the trajectory of the vermin, but still. I wasn't going to tell this stranger any of that. I still didn't take too kindly to strangers wearing couture and wingtips who looked like GQ models inside my leased small cabin.

I picked up my moose costume from the floor and returned it to the closet, suddenly feeling underdressed. The costume was warm, so I didn't need to wear clothes underneath. I glanced down and wiggled my toes. I did look ridiculous and, surprisingly, didn't care. I exuded confidence like my life coach, aka ladybug wannabe, had taught me. Except my boxers were sort of breezy and I didn't want to have a costume failure with my junk hanging out.

"If you'll excuse me," I said, "I think I should go put some pants on."

The guy lifted a perfectly trimmed brow. "Don't do that on my account." He gave me a wolfish grin that sent a shiver running down my spine. He had nice white teeth.

The better to eat you with.

Yeah, I had a horribly active imagination. It helped my writing but not so much my life. "I'll be back."

I headed to my bedroom in the loft. There was something strangely familiar about the man in my kitchen. It was one of those things that leeched onto my brain and wouldn't quite pull free. It had to be a picture, or maybe I imagined him. He could be a main character in one of my books. Tall, dark, strangely ominous, serial killer type. Yup. He could definitely belong in one of my novels. I quickly pulled on some jeans and a fraying gray sweater that hung loosely on my torso. I lived for comfort, not style. Sue me.

I returned to the kitchen, ignoring the man checking out the rainbow-colored socks I had kept on my feet. They were warm. "Did someone die?" I finally blurted, positioning myself behind the kitchen counter to separate us. I had full access to my knives should he pull a move on me. The smirk on his face vanished, replaced with a constipated look. I couldn't stop now that my interest was piqued. "Is someone suing me? You look like a harbinger of bad news."

If I didn't know any better, I'd say he let out a relieved breath as if he thought I figured something out about him I shouldn't have. Okay, I had to get a grip on my rambling mind.

"I don't know how to respond to that," he said dryly.

"Well, why are you here?"

"May I have a glass of water?"

An avoidance tactic—water. Yeah, I had played that card plenty of times with Sheriff Swanky. Since I was also thirsty and sweaty, I brought down two tall glasses from the cupboard and placed them on the counter. "Would you like tea instead?"

"Water is fine," he said.

If he thought I had fancy water, he was wrong. I turned the faucet on, and the walls started to tremble and shudder. It sounded as if a banshee had been set loose inside the walls until the faucet sneezed. Water shot out in bursts of three intervals before a steady stream spilled out. I gave him a smirk. "You gotta love the bucolic life, Thomas. I hope you've had your tetanus shot." Before I betrayed my composure and busted out laughing, I turned to the fridge and pulled out a store-bought bottle of cold tea.

"On second thought," Thomas said, "tea is fine."

I poured the tea. "So, Mr…"

"Raine."

I arched my brow. "Thomas Raine, that sounds made up." I pushed the tea across the counter toward him.

With that same smirk I was sure worked to pick up ladies and drop panties, he sipped the tea. His tongue darted out between his lips to capture the moisture there. A slow movement I couldn't help but notice for some god-awful reason. Okay, so maybe I'd been on bare minimum for five years. I hadn't had a sexual experience since Layla that didn't include Mr. Righty. That I even referred to it as a sexual experience made me wonder how the hell I made money as a romance author.

I took a long gulp of tea, avoiding eye contact with any part of his face as I did so. I wiped my lips with the back of my hand very unceremoniously and tapped the counter with my fingers. A nervous twitch I could never get rid of. I also noticed that he did not deny the fake name comment. Surprisingly, it didn't make me want to run for the hills. Instead, it made me curious. I wanted to pick this man's brain, maybe learn a bit or two on how to be this suave and sexy. Did I just say sexy? No, I thought it. Not sure if that was better.

"Are you going to tell me who you are and why you were looking for me?"

"Do I make you nervous, Mr. Diaz?"

Yeah. He did. "Why do you say that?" Because I just had to ask.

"Your hands are jittery."

I looked down at my hands still tapping the counter and quickly withdrew them to my sides.

"And you keep looking at my lips. Do I have something on them?" He did that licking thing again.

Yeah, I looked.

I sucked on my tea for a good moment, then matched his sexy licking gesture with my own back of the hand swipe against my lips again before carefully placing the glass on top of the counter. "Nope. You're good. How can I help you?"

He narrowed his eyes slightly and cocked his head just a smidgeon, studying me. I couldn't look away from those ocean blue saucers he claimed to be eyes. They were mesmerizing like a vortex in the middle of the ocean, sucking you down into its depths to drown you. "Mr. Diaz?"

"Huh?"

"You don't remember me?"

I would've remembered him. This man had a neon sign that screamed don't forget me. No one in their right mind could ever forget this man. "I'm sorry. You might have gotten the wrong Eric."

He rubbed his chin, his nails clean and glossy. He was definitely a manicure-type guy. His fingers were long and delicate, and I wondered what he did for a living. I didn't ask. Not my business.

"I was interested in leasing the cabin once your lease ended. I had assumed Mrs. Owens had contacted you about my arrival."

Mrs. Owens. The cabin. Light bulb moment had me giving myself a mental kick. "Right, she called last week. I'm sorry. I totally forgot. She asked if I'd give you a tour of the place."

He nodded and got to his feet. I had to tilt my head up to look at him. He did not belong in a place like this, which had my innate creative brain battling against appropriate things to say. My creative brain won. "You don't seem like the type to be interested in a cabin with six hundred square footage and bad plumbing."

His eyes held a hint of mirth in them. "What type do I look like?"

Okay, since he gave me permission, I took that moment to slowly take him in. "Well, for starters, wingtips in backcountry snow. No way. Expensive Gucci suit—"

"Armani."

"—Armani suit with no layers of protection from wind or snow. Dangerous. And—" I finally reached his broad chest and felt my breath hitch up a notch as I lifted my gaze to his strong chin, sharp features, and those arresting eyes that I believed could drown me. "And your hands," I finally said like an idiot.

He lifted his hands in front of him and looked at them. "What about my hands?"

I reached for them and felt him stiffen slightly. Maybe he didn't like to be touched. Ignoring all sensibilities warning me to stop touching this stranger, I turned his hand palm up, and traced my fingertips along his long, smooth, uncalloused, and very clean, fingers. His hands felt really nice. I hadn't felt nice hands since Layla. I swallowed the lump in my throat and finally stopped defiling his hands. "They're too smooth and too clean." I showed him my own blunt, ugly, coarse hands. "See. Working the fireplace requires chopping wood. But I'm sure you have people to do that for you, right?" I was rambling again and had to stop.

"I'm sure I can take care of my wood," he said. His voice took on a deeper, edgy sound and his eyes turned darker.

He was a wolf and I the sheep.

I blinked away the visual of him tearing my sheep throat out and jumped when my phone started playing "Who Let the Dogs Out" in the closet. My vet's special ringtone. "Sorry, I have to get this." I rushed to the closet where I'd left my cell phone, grateful for the intrusion but wary of the news Dr. V was about to give me.

Chapter Three

Zane

I expected him to sprint up to the loft for privacy. Instead, he locked himself inside the closet. I chuckled. Couldn't help it. When my father had offered me a truce, I decided on this last-ditch attempt at finding myself, as my mother so eloquently put it, and had jumped at the opportunity to finally meet the man who dominated my waking thoughts.

I'd met him at a low point in his life. A crushing moment that had left him shattered. While he hadn't deserved what happened to him, I was complicit in my own pain. Marie was dead because of me. When I saw his desperate expression after the public break-up with his wife, I remembered the same expression on Marie right before she took off in her Mercedes and crashed into a tree. I panicked. I couldn't let him leave. Something inside of me had awoken. Something dangerous, controlling, and possessive I couldn't ignore. I ran after him, caught him near his car, and practically kidnapped him.

He'd slept for most of it. Sobbed for the other. In his distress, I found my own release. Misery loves company. While we were both miserable in each other's arms, I had found something more. A nudging feeling that this straight, awkward man was the one for me. My family be damned.

Except he didn't remember me like I remembered him. Although we shared the same experience, he obviously didn't experience it the way I had. The thought made me crazed. I should leave. He was too good to be with me. I was a killer dressed in an Armani suit with wingtips. Arrogant, controlling, and possessive. I didn't deserve him. I'd only ruin him, and I couldn't do that. Not to him. The reason I'd given him an alias. So he could never find me.

Eric walked out of the closet looking as if he'd lost his best friend. "I'm sorry. There's been an emergency and I have to go."

I let out a relieved breath. Took it as a sign that fate was releasing me of my insane moment. In my defense, I'd accomplished what I set out to do. I learned that Eric Diaz was alive and well. He was obviously living the way he chose. His income afforded him nice things and yet he chose to live the bucolic life, paying for his sons' college tuitions. He also gave to various non-profits. Eric didn't seem to want fame. He just wanted to live. I respected that. So, I decided to leave and never look him up again. To put my feelings, real or imagined, back into its dark box behind my soul where I'd left my other pains of life. I'd accept the marriage proposal with the Rushmore family, merging the bloodlines. It would give us a position of greater power against the rising malice threat. I'll have an heir, won't unleash hell on earth, and humans could live happily without ever realizing that their world was a battleground for something much more malevolent than me. Except that the sad expression Eric wore tore at my insides and the words that subsequently spilled out of my mouth would be my undoing.

"Is there anything I can help you with?" Usually, that wasn't said with any type of sincerity. Just being polite. Like asking someone in passing how they were doing. You didn't expect them to stop and tell you their life story. You expected them to lie and tell you everything was fine and dandy so you could go on your way.

I should've known better.

"Actually, yeah," he said. "You can." He must've seen something in my expression that negated my offer because he quickly added, "I mean, if your ask is sincere. I don't want to impose."

Shit. "Of course it's sincere. What do you need?"

Eric pulled on a puffer coat and shoved his bright-colored socked feet inside snow boots. "I'll tell you on the way. I'll drive."

As I walked out of the cabin, I knew Bennett was going to be pissed. This was a security nightmare. I had expected to be in and out of this place, so I hadn't quite masked my arrival. I'd taken our private jet and used Thomas Raine, one of my aliases, to book the flight and a hotel stay. I usually traveled with at least three guards, but I had convinced Bennett I'd be safe. The truck in front of me was anything but safe. A dinosaur being eaten by rust. A splinter would have me dying of blood poisoning. Sad to say, that was one way I *could* die.

"What are you doing?" Bennett asked, taking his stubborn security specialist tone.

"He needs a favor."

Bennett arched a brow. Eric took that moment to walk out of the cabin and gave Bennett a beaming smile that filled me with jealousy.

"Oh," Eric said. "He could come too, but you'll have to sit in the back," he said to me. Without waiting, he jumped into the truck.

"I don't like this," Bennett grumbled and hopped into the passenger side while I stared at the back bench seat.

"I'm not going to fit back here," I said.

Eric turned and blushed. After we played one round of musical chairs, Bennett drove. I sat in the passenger seat while Eric sat in the back giving Bennett directions on how to get to his vet. Eric didn't elaborate on the condition of the dog. Leaning forward with his chin on his wrist on the back of my seat he looked at Bennett. "What's your name?"

"My apologies," I said. "This is Bennett. He's my driver."

"You don't know how to drive?"

I bit my lip to keep from smiling. Though it probably was a fair question, it wasn't one ever directed at me. "Yes. I know how to drive."

"Then why the driver? Do you not like driving? Or do you prefer someone to open the door for you?"

Bennett chuckled, then masked it with a cough. "I like ordering people around," I said with an edge to my voice I tried not to project. "Bennett takes orders really well."

Bennett glowered at me. I took that as a win.

Eric smiled. "So you guys are friends. That's nice. My friend tried killing me by asphyxiation today."

I bristled until I realized he meant the ladybug. "What was the deal with that, anyway?" Bennett asked.

"That's Rosa. We volunteer reading to kids at the library in costume. She wanted to get into my package."

I suddenly wanted to rip Rosa's head off her shoulders. Bennett must've sensed it and kept talking. "Package?"

"My advance readers copy of my next book. She wanted to read it before it came out."

"And why would you not want her to read it?"

"I added a character that mirrored her in the book and accidentally told her so now she's going to be fishing through it to see which one is her. I preferred to wait until I'm far from Maine when she finds out."

"That bad, huh?"

"I took the liberty of embellishing a little bit."

I caught the smile in his profile and my heart warmed considerably dangerous to tingling. Bennett glanced at me with a curious expression, and I realized I was smiling like an idiot. I quickly corrected myself.

We reached the veterinarian without incident. Eric looked troubled. "I just need help carrying her out. She's going to be sedated." He looked from me to Bennett. "I hope that's okay." For the first time since I met the man this morning, he looked unsure of himself. A glimpse of how he'd been when I first met him.

"Of course," I said.

He offered a slight nod and disappeared behind the counter. I already knew what Bennett was thinking, though my gifts did not include mind reading. "This was not the plan."

"I know."

"We are overstepping and cannot remain here."

"I know," I said a little bit too harshly, earning a pair of eyeballs aimed my way from the young receptionist. I smiled, pushing good thoughts her way, and she practically melted, returning to whatever she was doing. "Just give me some space."

"You know I cannot do that."

"Yes, you can." I glared at him. "No one will find me here." I knew I was losing the guy. Despite our decades of friendship and him giving up everything to protect me, I trusted him. Trusted his insight and judgment. "Do you sense a threat in him?"

Bennett snorted. "Maybe to the ladybug."

I pinched my lips to keep my smile in check. "Exactly."

Bennett sighed. "Fine. But I won't be far."

I nodded and he walked out.

Chapter Four

Eric

"I'm so sorry, Eric. We can only keep her comfortable."

I'd known this eventuality would happen. I'd adopted Boomer from the shelter knowing she had cancer. I'd picked her out of the others because she'd been scheduled to be euthanized. She'd been hiding in a corner, and my heart had melted at the sight of her. She hung on for four months, longer than the vets had anticipated. She loved the coast and chasing after the critters in the forest. She loved bacon treats, and slept on my bed. I hadn't once felt alone with her at my side. I should've protected my heart better. Falling in love had been too damn easy. Dr. V's hand squeezed my shoulder. "You did good with her, Eric."

I wiped away a tear and nodded. "Can I take her home?"

Doc handed me a brochure to a pet burial service. I shoved it into my pocket and walked out. I searched the waiting room for Bennett as I approached Thomas. "Where's your friend?"

"He took an Uber to the hotel. Why?"

"Oh, I thought he could carry Boomer."

"I could carry Boomer."

I wiped my nose and looked at the guy's well-fitted

suit. "I don't think you're dressed for it."

He cocked his head, making me feel all kinds of itchy inside. "I can carry her."

I led him to where Boomer was sleeping on her bed. She lifted her head and whimpered. Before I could touch her, Thomas had put his hand on top of her head in a warm gesture that heated all my insides. I'd never had a friend outside of family before, and I suddenly realized what I'd missed. Boomer warmed into him, and he carefully lifted the Labrador as if she weighed nothing.

"Lead the way," he said.

I quickly led him to the truck where we carefully put her on his lap, and then drove home. He kept sliding his hand along her coat in a soothing gesture easing her. A humming vibrated from his chest. A tune I didn't recognize that had even me feeling a bit relaxed too. I lowered my eyes to his left hand and realized he didn't wear a wedding ring, then admonished myself for looking. Why did I care if he was married or not? I didn't. "So did you decide on the lease?"

"Excuse me?" he asked. An adorable crease between his brows pinched his features.

"The lease. The reason you came to the end of the world."

He shook his head slightly. "I haven't decided what I'm going to do yet."

"Well, it may be a small, old thing in need of work, but nothing a good hand couldn't take care of." I smiled and could've sworn his ears turned a bit pink. "So what do you do for a living?" This was me trying to spark a conversation.

"Merger and Acquisitions."

"What does that even mean?"

"It means I buy companies and either keep them or sell them off."

"Oh, that sounds like it hurts."

"Not to me," he said in a way that made him seem more dangerous than I thought. Not the serial killer, knife to the gut dangerous, but the getting what he wants and to hell with anyone in his way dangerous.

"What do you do?"

"Oh, I write romance novels." I waited for the laugh that usually accompanied my employment status. Didn't come.

"Is that why you travel so much?"

I arched my brow. "How do you know I travel so much?"

"Your lease will be up soon. It's an assumption. Am I correct?"

I shrugged. "Yeah. I have two adult boys in college and am no longer tethered to any one place, so." I shrugged again.

"What about the missus?"

"Divorced." I left out the gory details. With the way my day was going, I didn't think I could swallow my pride with the wedge in my heart from losing Boomer. "What about you? Kids? Wife? Family?"

"No. No. And I have nine brothers."

"Wow. I have four sisters and I thought that was big."

He chuckled and I liked the sound of it.

Boomer seemed to get her second wind as we reached the cabin. She jumped up and started licking the guy. I envied her at that moment. Wait. What? Nope, I did not. "Boomer," I scolded. "Behave."

That only set her up to lick faster, and she practically had the man pinned to the seat when I opened his door to get her out. On her four legs, she managed to walk to the cabin door. Thomas tried to run his fingers through his hair, but the drool made his hair stick up and his fingers stuck.

"Drool's worse than semen for the hair," I said.

He seemed to have had something stuck in his throat because he started choking on a laugh. I patted his back.

"I mean, there was that movie," I quickly tried to backtrack and not hit myself upside the head. Thomas continued to laugh as he headed to the cabin. I liked listening to him laugh. He didn't appear to be the type of person who laughed often.

"May I clean up?" he asked once we'd settled Boomer in front of the fireplace.

Despite the dog hair and drool on his expensive coat and not to mention the condition of his hair, he still looked handsome. I almost tripped at the last thought. "Yeah, sure, upstairs the door to the right of the bed." My bed. My bathroom. I quickly recapped my morning disaster to make sure I hadn't left anything inappropriate to see. I was a man, in my prime—okay maybe a bit past my prime, but lube came in handy, and I may have considered sex so may have purchased a few sample condoms. I had those items tucked in my side table drawer. Except for my collection of Lego figurines, I had left nothing out. Just an unmade bed and dog hair. I lived a Spartan life. Easier to move around and hide from anyone trying to sell your organs.

I watched as he took the stairs to my private area. Heard his heavy footfalls and then the bathroom door closed. I panicked for good measure. "What's wrong with me?" I asked my dog.

Boomer didn't respond.

After my messy break-up, I'd lost myself. When I'd finally awakened from hell, every unnecessary item was purged from my life. Except for my boys, my laptop, and my books, I had nothing of value. Furniture, clothes...all of it. Layla had gone through a midlife crisis with her lover and abandoned our house and our boys. Sebastian had been thirteen at the time while Alejandro was sixteen. I had no choice but to live for them, which was a blessing, I suppose. After Sebastian graduated high school, I sold the house and rebuilt myself. I'd spent time in LA, Montana, Alaska, and did a stint in Puerto Rico. Small towns and away from people were my preference. People usually sucked. The time surrounding my break-up had been soul-crushing. Depression, heartbreak, and pain had flowed out of me in synergy with my stories. People loved a great tragedy that unrealistically ended in happily ever after. I never got my happily ever after. But I wasn't dead yet.

The house took that moment to come alive. The walls rattled and I heard a piercing scream from the upstairs bathroom.

Thomas.

With my heart wedged in my throat, I sprinted up the steps and into the bathroom to find a very naked Mr. Raine against the back wall of the shower avoiding the now scalding hot spray misting the bathroom at an alarming rate. Suds in his hair and eyes. "Fuck," he said. "The water got too hot."

I didn't register his words because, well, the guy was naked. I was distracted by all the lean muscles, pale

25

bare skin, and uncut appendage that hung obscenely long and thick despite the lack of erection.

"What the hell?" he spat out.

That brought me back to my senses. "It's okay. I have to adjust the water pressure in the basement. Just don't—" That's as far as I got when I was whipped off my feet and slammed against the wall hard enough to see stars. I heard Thomas swear as if I'd been ejected into another dimension. I heard Boomer barking and then saw a flash of glowing red eyes in front of me just before I passed out.

Chapter Five

Zane

Fuck!

I just caught the slight movement before Bennett slammed Eric against the wall. I lunged on instinct. All my primordial power rushed to the surface, heating every cell in my body as power generated through me in a chaotic loop that had me seeing red. I rammed against the big man, freeing Eric from his grasp. The urge to tear his head off his shoulders was so fucking potent, I had to bite down to keep from doing it with my teeth.

"Don't you ever fucking touch him," I growled out.

"I felt your distress," Bennett said quickly. "I thought he was hurting you."

Uh, just for that, I wanted to slowly slice the flesh from his bones. "Really? Really? You think he could best *me?*" I pulled a towel from the rack and wiped my stinging eyes just before I crouched next to Eric on the floor.

"Fuck. I'm sorry." Bennett went to pick up Eric, but I growled again, flashing my teeth. "If you ever touch him again, I will rip your spine from your body. Are we clear?" I rarely ever threatened anyone and, when I did, I wasn't fucking kidding. The look on Bennett's face said enough.

"Yeah, okay."

I cleared my head and listened to the steady beat of the human's heart and eased his pain receptors. He had no permanent damage. I suspected his passing out was more attributed to my own dispelling of melatonin to calm the fuck down before I put a crater in Bennett's face. I carried Eric to his bed and carefully laid him down.

"What do we do now?"

Damage control. I couldn't very well tell Eric the truth. That I was born of an immortal race subjugated to walk the earth for eternity. That my enhanced powers included manipulating the design of the world to fit whatever the fuck I wanted. Though never to be used unless saving the race from intruders. And humans were one fucking big intruder in my world. "I'll figure it out. Just go."

Without a word, the dumbass disappeared. I knew he was still close. I also knew he would never touch Eric without permission *ever* again. I ran my fingers along his forehead, moving the strands of curls away from his face. The man was beautiful and so not my type. He was gentle, honest, kind, and generous with his heart and things. Shit. Me being here was so damn wrong, but I couldn't leave. I had twenty-four hours, and I was going to use them. He stirred, then his eyes fluttered open, and he blinked. Then he jolted to a sitting position, almost knocking me on my forehead.

"The water. Are you okay? Ohmygod, please tell me you didn't burn yourself."

The fact that he was worried about me after passing out made me wish I were someone else. Anyone that could stay by his side. "I'm fine. You slipped on the floor in the bathroom and hit your head."

He rubbed the back of his head trying to remember. I didn't have the power to alter memory, only emotions. And I wasn't going to mess with his. Not if I didn't have to.

"Yeah, right." He seemed to come out of his haze and looked at me. I remembered how he had stared at me in the shower. It made me wonder if he saw me worthy of at least a kiss. I threw that thought away as soon as it emerged. Kisses were dangerous. I never kissed a lover. Ever.

He threw his legs over the side of the bed and got to his feet. "I'll, uh, go fix the water pressure so you can, uh, finish up."

Before I could say anything, he headed back downstairs. A few moments later, he called the all-clear to finish showering. After a few moments, I heard a soft tap on the door.

"You can come in," I called out.

I heard him just beyond the shower curtain. "I didn't think you'd want to wear your suit so I left some joggers and a tee-shirt that might fit."

"Okay, thanks. I'll call Bennett to bring me some clothes before I go."

"Oh," I heard him say. "Okay." Then the door shut.

Once finished, I picked up the black tee-shirt he left me and put it to my nose. It smelled like him. Woodsy with a hint of citrus. A sudden jolt of desire rushed through me, imprinted with that scent. *His* scent. I quickly dressed and climbed down the stairs.

He was soothing Boomer when he saw me and smiled at me. "Everything good?" he asked.

I wasn't sure if he meant us or the clothes. Both

were good so I just nodded. He got to his feet and washed his hands in the sink. "I have sandwiches if you're hungry."

I was starving but not for food. "That'd be great."

"Did you get to call Bennett for your clothes?"

"Yeah. He'll be here as soon as he can."

"Sorry about the water. Had I known you meant to shower, I would've adjusted the temperature for you."

"It was my fault. I should've asked."

"Well, you did help me with Boomer, so whatever you need that I can provide is yours."

That was something Eric should not have offered. In my world, word was law. Offers were sacred, and vows honored in blood. But Eric wasn't part of my world. Not yet. "You probably shouldn't offer yourself so freely. You don't know what I'm capable of asking for."

That threw the man off guard. I hated that I couldn't get a read on him. His emotions were always all over the place. Like looking through a kaleidoscope, the colors of his aura creating indiscernible shapes that made no sense. Some melded together while others took off on their own. When I first met him, I thought the arrays had something to do with his heartbreak. But now, it seemed this was his frame of mind all the time. It left me absorbing more than I needed.

A spark of curiosity crossed the man's expression. "And what would you ask for that would shock me?"

"Oh, your soul, your firstborn, your body?" Too bad he seemed to favor having the kitchen counter between us.

"I'd trade my body for yours anytime."

The guy was fucking adorable. Naïve and maybe

too innocent for me, but damn adorable. "I could tell by the way you looked at me when I was in the shower." Yeah, I went there.

He blushed. It took centuries of training to control my urges and not to reach out and taste those damn full lips of his. "Yeah, um, sorry about that."

"Don't apologize. I like that you looked."

He swallowed nervously. "Are you hitting on me?"

Holy, hell. If this guy only knew what I was doing. "Is it working?"

"I'm not gay," he said quickly.

Something I expected him to say and had been waiting for. I slowly walked around the counter, invading his space until I had his back pressed against the wall. He didn't move or reach to touch me. I leaned into him and inhaled him. My body responded with need and something else. An underlying warning to stay the fuck away from him. Ignoring that rational part, I grazed my lips along his jaw and made a trail to his ear. "It isn't about a label, Mr. Diaz," I said, noticing the goosebumps rising along his neck. "It's a visceral reaction of the body. A hormonal response. Tell me." I edged my lips against his strong jaw feeling the heat of him through the narrow space between us. "How does your body feel right now?"

He opened his mouth to speak when someone started pounding on the door. He seemed relieved. "I, uh, should get that."

As the moment shattered and my prize rushed toward the door, I decided to end Bennett's life. Except it wasn't Bennett at the door, but the ladybug from earlier.

Rosa.

And she wasn't wearing her costume.

Killing her would be a good placeholder for Bennett especially since she wrapped her arms around Eric's neck and hugged him tight. "I'm so sorry, honey," she said.

The term of endearment had me grinding my teeth.

"I'm okay. I'll be okay," he said into her neck, but Eric didn't sound convincing, and I realized what a jerk I'd been. Spewing shit about sex while his dog was dying. I should've offered an emotional connection. Empathy. Something. Instead, I made it about me.

She broke the connection and gave Boomer some attention. "What did the doctor say?"

"A few days. We can only make her comfortable now."

She kissed the dog and eased her back down. "I'm sorry, baby," she whispered. Then she got up to face Eric. "You did really good with her. You know that, right?"

He shrugged and shoved his hands into his pockets. No, I didn't think Eric realized any good thing he'd ever done.

Rosa opened her mouth, then shut it when she saw me. "And why is he still here? And wearing your clothes. Did you two have sex?"

"Rosa!" Eric admonished. I liked the shade of pink lifting to his face. "That's none of your business."

He didn't quickly say no. That was something to file for later inspection.

"Ohmygod, you're blushing. You did have sex. Finally. Though, I didn't know you were into men, but hey, I do not judge."

Eric rolled his eyes as he dropped onto the sofa.

"Oh, God, you're giving me a headache."

"So who is your new lover?" she asked, walking toward me.

"Thomas Raine," I answered.

She turned to Eric who remained on the sofa. "Are you bringing him to the dance?"

"No," Eric said dryly.

"The sheriff will be there."

"Hell no," he said.

She chuckled.

The mention of the sheriff got my attention. "What's this dance?" I asked. Not that I'd ever expected to be interested in going to a small-town dance. I couldn't say I'd ever been to one to judge.

"Oh, it's a fundraiser for our local library," Rosa said. "You should come."

I suddenly wanted to go.

"Rosa, he's a stranger," Eric said.

Rosa snorted. "Honey, he's wearing your clothes. I think the stranger danger of whatever this is"—she waved her hand between us—"already left the building."

I liked Rosa.

"Did you want to go?" Rosa asked me.

I shrugged. "Sure. I'm in town until tomorrow."

Rosa turned and plopped Eric a kiss on his forehead. "I'll see you there." Then she handed me a flyer with the information. "Make sure he doesn't chicken out." Rosa gave me a wink and walked out.

Chapter Six

Eric

Bury me now. Just put me out of my misery. As an introvert and an artist with a wild imagination, I craved normalcy. No, not normalcy, for invisibility. I was okay with being forgotten. Hell, no one knew who the hell I was in high school. My family couldn't say if they'd seen me at a family gathering or not. I was okay with that. Not being noticed.

So why the hell did I attract Rosa Reyes into my life. The woman just acknowledged the elephant in the room with a roar.

Did I have sex with Thomas?

I almost snorted. First off, I was not interested in men despite his spiel about listening to my body. Okay, so I'd gotten hard at his nearness, but that was because I'd been on bread and water for the past five years and he was all sexual innuendos and prowess. I'd never been attracted to a man before, and Thomas was different. Yeah, he was a man. But…there was something more about him. And I was curious. And secondly, why the hell would he be interested in me? I was nothing. At least ten years his senior. Wore a moose costume to hide my fear as I read to children at the public library. I wore mismatched socks. Said the wrong things at the wrong time. And I was not the type for a man like Thomas Raine. A fake name if ever I heard one.

"Are you okay?"

The sound of his deep, erotic voice reminded me just how lacking in the sex department I'd been. I shifted in my seat. "Sorry about her. She's a tsunami."

"I actually like her spirit."

I snorted. "Yeah, you can call it that."

"If you'd rather I not go—"

I got up from the sofa. "No. I mean yes. Go. If you want. But don't be obliged to go on my account." I wished he'd reconsider and not go so I could hide out with Boomer all night.

"I'm good with going. My flight doesn't leave until tomorrow morning, so I'm pretty much free."

The thought of him leaving left an ache in my chest. Of course he was leaving. He was not a friend or lover or whatever the hell my broken imagination thought him up to be. He'd come to visit the cabin, decide if he wanted to lease it, and then leave. Not to save me from my moose costume, carry my dog, or go with me to this darn fundraiser. Yet, he did. He was. An enigma. One I'd seen naked and now had to sear my eyeballs to get the image out of my head. I was going to hell. Thankfully, Bennett took that moment to pound on the door and drop off Thomas's clothes. A few minutes later, he was dressed in dark jeans, boots, and a cardigan that accented his very muscular physique. Yeah, who was I kidding? I noticed.

"What time should I pick you up?" he asked, throwing on a puffer jacket also brought by his driver.

"You really don't have to do this."

He lifted the flyer. "I was invited. So, I'll see you

there or we can go together. Your pick."

Stalker much?

"Four. Us party animals party before sundown."

The familiar smile burrowed a tingly sensation inside my gut. Nerves. I hated nerves. "Then I'll see you at four."

Then he was gone like a leaf on a gentle breeze. Well, more like a tumbleweed in a sandstorm. The weather did not feel conducive to partying. And it would snow soon. I locked the door behind him, checked on a sleeping Boomer, and retreated to my bathroom.

I couldn't get the image of Thomas naked out of my mind, and that was disconcerting. The man was beautiful, clothed, and unclothed. By his attire and having his own personal driver, I knew he had money. I also knew he wanted me in ways I couldn't imagine. Which made me feel fragmented. It scared and excited me. He made me feel something I missed with Layla. In control of the chaos around me. He hadn't touched me when he had me pinned to the wall as if he anticipated the first move would be mine. I'd never had much control in my relationship with Layla. She ordered my life. She made it easy by making all the decisions, paying the bills and running the household. All I had to do was provide the income and the occasional orgasm and everything worked out. Until it hadn't, and I had to figure shit out for myself. Paying bills, making doctor appointments, and trying to make ends meet because I hadn't sued her for child support, afraid that she would then take the boys away from me. I knew the family courts always leaned toward giving custody to the mother. And Layla wasn't a bad mom. She just wanted something else. *We* weren't that something else.

So I did everything on my own. I took control and it had felt thrilling and scary as hell.

The same emotions now with Thomas. Although he was clearly the alpha in any relationship, I felt as if he wanted to give me control. Except I didn't intend on acting on it. I wasn't gay. And despite how my cock reacted, I could never be with a man that way. It wasn't me.

After showering, I realized Thomas had used the towel hanging on the bar. Carefully, not to slip the way I had earlier, I stepped out of the tub and onto my mat. The mat that I had purchased after Boomer had slipped getting out of the bathtub. I'd purchased it for twelve ninety-nine and it covered the entirety of the small floor space so that I or Boomer would not slip and fall. So how the hell did I manage to slip and knock myself out cold like Thomas had said happened?

No way I could've slipped.

I rubbed the back of my head as I remembered the naked man in the bathtub. I had started to turn off the water when I'd been lifted off the floor and thrown against the wall. The last thing I remembered before passing out was Bennett and his red eyes.

No way. I was going crazy. Being alone with limited human interaction, I'd finally busted a vein in my brain and was going batshit. I hurried out and found a clean towel. My phone rang.

"I'm going nuts," I said to Rosa.

"I knew it. You had sex with him." Her voice practically squealed over the line.

Ohmygod, sometimes I wanted to strangle this one. "No. Why would you say something like that? I'm not gay."

"I thought you might be curious."

I rolled my eyes, though she missed the full effect of it. "You are nuts."

"I thought you said you were nuts."

"I am, but different from your warped brain."

"Hey, my warped brain has helped many a wayward mind to find their rightful place in the world."

"Jesus, are you sprouting your ad to me?"

"It's a good one. Thank you for that."

Uh, there was no hope for a healthy conversation with this one. "Why did you call?"

"I got Mindy to come out to stay with Boomer for the evening. She should be there at about four."

I let out a rushed breath. Mindy was Dr. V's assistant. "Thanks, Rosa. You are a doll, sometimes."

"More times than not," she said.

I agreed but didn't let her know that.

"So you have a date with this Thomas Raine, huh. I looked him up on Google. Found nothing on him. That's a good sign, right?"

"You are certifiable, missy."

"Hey, I'm looking out for you."

"Thanks. I have to get dressed. I have an hour."

"Right. I'll see you there. And, Eric…don't think I didn't notice that you did not deny the mention of dating Thomas Raine." Before I could put my two cents in it, she hung up.

Denying anything would've turned me into a rambling idiot. I had preferred silence. Whatever. Let her think whatever she wanted. My wardrobe needed my attention at the moment. Sadly, I had nothing in my closet that would compete with how well Mr. Raine was going to look, I was sure. Chinos were my favorite dress-up slacks. No iron, easy wash. I pulled on the black ones with a white button-down and a dark blazer. That was all the dress-up clothes in my possession. I tousled my hair with curly hair products to tame the frizz, shaved off the stubble I'd been growing for the winter, and found myself staring at a forty-two-year-old single man with boyish features. What did I care? I didn't. *Yeah, right, buddy. Keep telling yourself that.*

I headed toward my ringing door to let Mindy inside. Boomer was happy to see her. I was relieved and instructed her to call me if she needed me back here. I also asked her to report to me at least every hour. She threw me out of the house when Thomas's sedan drove up to the cabin. Bennett driving. And his eyes were not red.

That was a good sign.

Chapter Seven

Zane

We reached the cabin just as Eric was opening the door. I felt a tinge of disappointment having him meet me at the car. I'd wanted to pick him up in the traditional date sense. I'd never been on one before and thought it was the norm. Until I remembered this wasn't a date.

"Just enjoy tonight. We leave tomorrow," Bennett said.

We hadn't spoken about his slip-up with Eric, nor the reason behind my response to scalding hot water against my skin. Yeah, I had screamed and yeah, I had thought hell had finally caught up to me. Bennett had responded accordingly, except that he had threatened Eric and the man was *mine*. Not to be harmed. Ever.

Eric looked good in plain black chinos, boots, and a pea coat that didn't seem to work against the wind picking up, messing up his curly hair. He'd shaved, and it drew even more attention to his full lips.

"Remember, you haven't claimed him, so don't kill anyone should he have a significant other in the party. I will not be happy if I have to clean up *your* mess," Bennett said.

I gave him my middle finger. He chuckled.

Eric got into the car. The cold followed him inside

until he shut the door. I got an instant whiff of his scent and every cell in my body awakened to it. Fuck. This was not good. Scent memory was more powerful than vision or emotions. And I'd inadvertently allowed his scent to cross the threshold into my essence. Something that could never be erased.

"I hate the cold," he said, rubbing his gloved hands together.

"You could always head south, away from the cold." *With me*. I didn't add.

"Is that where you live? South?"

"I go where the work takes me," I said honestly.

Eric didn't push it, and I offered nothing more. I'd already decided to head back home after my tryst with him. I'd leave nothing behind. Better not to give him clues to search me out. It'd be too dangerous for him.

The event was held at the local library hall. A small space decorated with pale color linens and hanging swirls of decoration. Okay, maybe tacky in my sense, but it seemed to please the locals, which I realized consisted of more females than males. Four, in particular, took an interest in Eric and me as we walked toward our assigned table at the front of the room. We didn't quite make it when Sheriff Swanky, wearing her sheriff uniform, stopped Eric. I didn't need to read minds to know Eric felt uncomfortable next to the woman who stood five feet nothing and still had an imposing attitude. She touched Eric's arm, leaving it there in a possessive gesture.

"And there she goes," Rosa said beside me. "She's a slut."

I followed the ladybug, now in a green dress, to the dessert table where three other women watched Eric

41

with the sheriff.

"I bet a hundred she's going to tap that ass," a platinum blonde said.

Rosa snorted. "Not on your life, Trudy."

I wanted to drown Trudy in the punch bowl.

"He's too good for her," another auburn-haired woman said. She had dreamy green eyes aimed at Eric. I clenched my hands into tight fists to keep them steady. Bennett was right. I should not be here. Eric was not mine. But if he went home with any of these women, I would not be responsible for what happened to them. The demon inside me would demand retribution. Consequences be damned.

"Here," Rosa said, handing me a red solo cup with an amber liquid. "It's spiked. Looks like you need it."

The cheap booze must've left a hole in my gut. It sat in my stomach like a stone. "So what brings you to Moose Hills," the blonde said, wrapping her arm around mine. Surprisingly, I didn't sense evil in the wench. Too bad.

"Just passing through. Thought about renting Owen's cabin."

The three women snorted. "That thing is a fire hazard. I'm surprised Eric hasn't met his demise in that piece of shit."

The thought of Eric hurt made me grind my teeth. At this rate, I'd be busting a flame that would send all these people writhing in agony. "May, did you fart?" Trudy asked the auburn-haired woman.

"Of course not, you harlot," May countered.

Eric took that moment to turn to me, and his eyes lowered to Trudy's arm wrapped around mine. For the briefest moment, I felt jealousy. Not mine. His. But it was fleeting and hard to hang on to, especially with Swanky pulling his attention to her.

"Okay, this is criminal enough," Rosa said, taking my arm. "Let's go save him."

She led me to Eric, who caught my gaze with a sense of relief. "Sheriff, please take your seat. The auction will be starting soon."

Swanky didn't seem pleased at being sent away from Eric, but Rosa didn't care. Eric reached for my arm and leaned into me. My shoulder brushed his chest, and his breath heated my neck. I was about to explode and take all these heathens with me.

"Don't leave me," Eric whispered into my ear.

Never. The thought struck me like a ton of bricks. We followed Rosa to our table near the stage.

"You really need to grow a pair of balls, Diaz," Rosa said.

"Whatever," Eric responded.

He sat between Rosa and me. "I don't know if I could outbid her," Rosa said.

"Oh, God, please. I'll give you the money back."

"It's not about the money, Eric. She'll give me parking tickets and hunt me down on the road. It's easier for you. You're leaving in a few months."

I felt lost and leaned into him, closer than I probably should have. I took in his scent again. It felt right. "What do you mean bid?"

"Fundraiser," he said. "You can bid on someone for a date with them this evening."

"Here," Rosa handed me her paddle. "Win Mr. Chino pants over here. I'm not going against Swanky."

Eric gave a long sigh.

"I'll win you," I said.

Eric turned to look at me, and our faces were just inches apart. He didn't pull away and I couldn't tell if the uptick in his heart rate had to do with our close proximity or fear of having to spend an evening with Swanky. "I'll repay you every penny and even pay for dinner."

I smiled and liked the way his eyes fell to my lips. "You will pay," I said.

His baby brown eyes widened. Before I could attempt to read into the way he leaned closer, his phone vibrated, tearing away the moment. I almost growled in frustration until he looked up with a sad expression and I remembered Boomer.

"Is she okay?" I asked.

"Yeah. I asked Mindy to give me a text every hour. I just want this over with so I can be with her."

So did I.

I put my hand on his thigh to reassure him, but he stiffened and looked as if he were about to start sprouting trivia information on moose. "I'll win you, then we'll pick up dinner on the way home."

He relaxed at my words and didn't correct me on the use of the word home. The cabin wasn't his home and it sure as hell wasn't mine. But it felt like home with him. A strange feeling overcame me and I had to push it away before I did release a toxin that would have everyone in this place crazed.

Rosa got to her feet. "Okay, let's do this."

The auction started with a tea date with Mrs. Bumbling, the mayor's wife, and ended with the onslaught of Sheriff Swanky. Eric raised ten thousand dollars all by his lonesome. What can I say? I had no time to stretch the auction. I wanted my man nice and neat. No one raised their paddle after my bid, and it was worth it just to see the shocked expressions of the locals and the blush creeping up Eric's cheeks. I had no idea if a *friend* would've spent so much for dinner, but I was beyond caring about etiquette.

Swanky gave me a sneering look and quickly stomped away from my playing ground. Eric returned to the table a bit winded. "I told you to win me, but you didn't have to bid so much."

"What can I say? I'm a generous guy. Now let's get out of here."

Eric rolled his eyes. "More like an impatient one," he grumbled.

"I heard that."

Bennett dropped us off at the cabin and I sent him away before hopping into Eric's truck and driving to the local burger joint, which were aplenty in this neck of the woods. Eric had already called the order in when we were in the car. He just wanted to relieve Mindy quickly and spend some time with Boomer. It wasn't until I headed back to the truck after picking up the two bags of food that every cell in my body erupted in chaos. As if the links keeping me together had suddenly started to stretch and would snap at any moment, tearing me out of existence in the process. The world shifted under me, and pain coated the walls I'd carefully erected to protect my soul. I fell to my knees and fought for control. Fought to stitch the crack in the seam around the darkness inside of me.

Eric's scent consumed me. He was in excruciating pain, and I felt it a thousand-fold.

I shut my eyes and breathed, sensing a presence I hadn't felt in years.

"You totally fucked up now."

I would've heard him laughing if my ears weren't still ringing. I managed to claw my way to my feet, using the truck for purchase, and opened the driver's door. I shoved the bags inside and climbed in, praying that Eric was still safe and sound where I'd left him in the cabin.

There would be hell to pay if anyone hurt him. And I knew all about hell.

Chapter Eight

Eric

Boomer took her last breath and laid still. Too still. I knew this day would come, but it seemed too soon. Four months wasn't enough time to be with her, and I had been the fool to give her all the love I couldn't give anyone else. As pathetic as it sounded, she had been the reason I left the cabin to go on long walks. The reason I'd learned to love this space, the woods, and the small town. I'd never felt as if I belonged anywhere, and I had searched aplenty. Refusing to settle down in one place for too long because of this very moment. Losing someone you loved.

I couldn't move from the spot on the floor beside her. Her head resting on my lap. My heart shattered and I couldn't stop the sobs racking out of my body. It sounded obscene in the silent space. There was no preparing for death. I was a fool to think otherwise.

The lock turned and the door opened. Thomas walked inside, left the bags on the counter, and rushed toward me. His hair was winded, his cheeks red from the cold, and he looked so handsome.

He dropped to his knees but didn't move to touch me, just placed a hand on top of Boomer's head.

"I thought I was ready for this," I said between sobs. "I...I thought I made it better for her."

He cupped my face, and I appreciated the contact. His hands were unusually warm. The touch sent a wave of calmness through me when all I wanted to do was curse the world. "You did, baby," he said. The term of endearment made me feel all kinds of things I wasn't ready for. "You made her happy until the end. And you were always with her."

I nodded like an idiot. As if I really believed I did make a difference for her. I wanted to believe that. "Can you call the burial service? The number is on the counter. I'm going to shower."

He nodded and gently helped me move Boomer's head onto her bedding. Then he helped me to my feet. His touch was gentle, his presence soothing. I left him in the kitchen and sauntered to the loft and into the bathroom. Sitting on the toilet seat, I felt numb. I'd always been hypersensitive. Especially as a child. I felt emotions in spades. I could never attend a funeral. I cried during all the Disney movies I had watched with my boys and cried through three months of my life after Layla left me.

And the emotions never ended with sadness. It blended with rage, fear, guilt, all in spades. The reason I learned to lead a moral life. Nothing to rage about, nothing to fear, and nothing to feel guilty for. I'd done nothing wrong. So why did it feel as if the world was crushing me? Boomer was in a better place. She'd no longer suffer the way she had in this world. I knew that in my soul. The living carried the weight of the dead. I knew that too. But it didn't lessen the sting, the pain of being left behind. I rubbed my neck at the echo of pain still lingering there. It did nothing to ease my shame. *That* I felt in spades.

I lifted my eyes to Thomas standing in the doorway. I hadn't even heard him come up the stairs. "They said they can be here within the hour."

I nodded. Unable to sound my thanks. I couldn't move. My body felt heavy, numb. I didn't know how to feel anymore. I expected Thomas to walk away. To run, really. He'd paid ten thousand dollars for the date from hell. But instead, he approached me and dropped to his knees. Then he started taking off my shoes. He lifted my leg so he could pull them out with my socks. Then the other. I was made into a puppet, and he was my master. And I didn't care. After my shoes were neatly placed just outside the small bathroom, he started slowly unbuttoning my shirt. Gave me enough leeway to tell him to stop. To tell him I was an adult and didn't need his help to undress and shower. I've been doing that by myself for at least thirty-nine years. Give or take. But I said nothing. Just stared at his stoic expression. The clear ocean blue eyes that seemed to change colors like a mood ring. I'd have to remember all his moods for reference. His features were relaxed, his lips pressed softly together. The man had no hint of stubble. If memory served me correctly, he had no hair on his body either.

He slipped his fingers up along my chest, pushing the shirt off my shoulders and slowly pulling on the folded sleeves, leaving me in my white undershirt. Then he met my eyes and didn't look away as his fingers inched up the seam of the tee, skimming my stomach as he pulled it over my head, dropping it in the corner. My body flamed. My heart unsettled as thoughts rattled inside me with nothing but the look of this man in front of me to ground me. A man who came like a shadow in the night and stayed with me. It had actually been early morning, but details didn't matter. What mattered was that he was still here in my moment of need.

Then his hands trailed my bare shoulders, sending sparks along their path. His fingers ran down my chest and rubbed against my hardened nipples. My body paid attention along with my cock, which was pressed painfully behind the zipper of my pants. I wanted to touch him but found I couldn't quite move. I wanted to narrow the gap between us and kiss him but couldn't draw enough nerve to go that far. Afraid that he would reject me. Afraid that I'd do this all wrong. Afraid that my feelings, my need, weren't real. I'd never felt this way for a man. A *man*.

After a few moments of utter silence, he got up and turned on the water.

"I adjusted the water for you," he said. His voice thick and deep.

Thank you, I thought. I still couldn't speak. Afraid that despair would consume me again.

"Do you want me to help you undress?"

Yes. I would like you to help me forget my life. I shook my head instead.

"I'll be right outside. Just let me know if you need anything. Can you do that?"

I nodded. He walked out, closing the door to give me some privacy but leaving it open a sliver so he could hear my call should I choose to invite him into my body.

I wanted to invite him in. I just wasn't so sure what that meant, exactly. Yeah, I'd researched the shit out of sex for my books, but it'd never been real. It'd never been *my* emotion. And in reality, I feared all of it.

I undressed and let the hot spray cleanse my body until I was raw. After the shower, I dressed in a pair of PJ bottoms and sat at the edge of the bed waiting for the burial service to arrive. Thomas opened the door for them as I remained in my room, unable to watch them take Boomer. A few minutes after they left, I slipped under the covers. Thomas entered the room after a few more long minutes, then slipped into the bathroom to shower. Afterward, he climbed into bed behind me, and I let him spoon me. His bare chest against my back. My ass against his obvious erection. I almost wished he'd do something. Kiss me. Touch me. Make me feel something other than useless. I was pathetic. That much was made clear the moment Layla left me.

Instead, I heard his breathing deepen and soft snores behind me. I waited a little bit more, feeling his even breaths against my neck and his fast heartbeat against my back until nothing was left and I dropped away from this world and into sleep.

Chapter Nine

Zane

After the men left with Boomer, I cleaned the dog's fluids from the floor. Death was always messy whether you died of natural causes or a knife to the throat. I was used to wet work, though I rarely did it and never enjoyed it.

I spoke with Bennett after Eric had gone to shower. He'd felt my distress at the diner but after I'd threatened him, he decided that a slight slip up in the form of a massive emotional intrusion was not life-threatening, he ignored it. At least until I told him about sensing Finnegan, Lucifer's eldest son and wraith. The fucker made it his life goal to make my life a living hell. And we were both immortal.

That had Bennett spewing a few more curse words of the likes to embarrass Lucifer himself. The devil did have a mouth on him. A beautiful, evil mouth. I sent Bennett on a mission to figure out what the fuck Finn was doing in this realm and told him I was staying the night with Eric.

"Get it out of your system and get your ass back in line, Zane. You don't need this shit right now. Especially not if Finnegan is on the prowl," Bennett warned before disconnecting the call.

I knew that. I just had to get Eric out of my system.

Fuck them and leave them. That was me. Nothing else.

I had considered heading out but couldn't stop this feeling overpowering everything else. The need to ensure Eric's safety. To know he'd be okay. His vulnerability pushed all my buttons. It hadn't been the plan. His obvious visceral response to me didn't make leaving him any easier. Thank the Fates that he hadn't accepted my proposition of fully undressing him. It would've led to more. Except, that didn't stop me from crawling into bed behind him. Just to sleep. I reasoned. Just until morning. Falling asleep had just happened. I hadn't slept this soundly since right before my father had sent me to hell. Literally. To enhance my education with Lucifer himself. All angels were androgynous, and they flipped both ways when the occasion called for it. Lucifer was no different. More insatiable, conceited, and totally self-centered, but who was I to criticize.

I woke up just before dawn in the exact position I'd fallen asleep. During the night, Eric had turned to face me. He'd burrowed his face into my chest. His arm around my waist, one leg propped between my thighs. He smelled of soap and shampoo underneath his own scent that had become part of me. I inhaled him. The shift had him stirring, and he grazed his groin against my thigh. His erection was as solid as mine.

Don't do it, asshole. The reasonable side of my brain ordered.

You only have one night. The night's over. Do it now or never. He wants you.

No, he doesn't. He's vulnerable because of his loss. Do not take advantage of him.

I was at war with myself. All of my doubt shattered when he nudged my leg aside, scooting closer so there was no space between our bodies. He slipped his hand inside the waistband of my briefs and cupped my ass, drawing me closer to his need. To *my* need. I fisted the back of his hair and pulled his head back to look into his face. To be sure he was fully awake for this. That he wanted this as much as I did. His eyes fluttered open. They were amazingly lighter, like amber with specks of gold in them.

Beautiful.

I licked his throat and trailed up along his chin to his ear. "I need to know that you want this." I knew he was still half asleep, but I didn't give a fuck. He'd regret it when I was gone, but I needed his consent like I needed to breathe him in. "Say it, baby. I'll make you forget yourself."

He licked his lips, and I avoided them at all costs. No kisses. Kisses were too intimate, too dangerous. I already took his scent into my essence; I couldn't take half his soul. "Make me forget myself," he whispered. "Please."

The pathetic piece of shit that I was, I took that as assent. I pushed him back onto the bed, got up on my knees, and tore the covers off him. The body laid out before me was perfect. He wasn't built like my other partners. He had a thin build, narrow waist and hips, but bred out of lack of eating, of regular life activities rather than hitting the gym. I ran my hand down his chest, his stomach, all of him smooth and soft. My fingers dipped under the seam of his PJ bottoms and lowered them with his briefs. Freeing his cock, it bobbed against his stomach. Hard, smooth, long, and uncut.

My mouth watered at the sight of it. Of him

watching me peruse all of him.

"Thomas," he said. I hated the lie of my name on his lips. I wanted to hear my true name when I brought him over the brink. But my real name on his lips would shatter my already confused heart. "Thomas," he said again. Pleading.

I frantically shoved my pants down, and kicked them off, then slotted our bodies together. He made a noise at the back of his throat, chasing the friction with me. Lips parted, moaning in pleasure, his eyes half-lidded—the man was beautiful. "I don't know what I'm doing."

"You're perfect, baby. Just do what feels good." I inhaled his human pheromones of arousal.

He nodded and moaned as I continued to rock against him. I lifted myself and took both our cocks in my hand, tugging at our length, creating a delicious friction that sent us both into pleasure. He moaned deep. The urge to bite his exposed throat had my mouth watering.

"That feels so good," he said. His eyes closed.

"Open your eyes," I ordered. He quickly locked his eyes to mine. "I want you to see who's fucking you."

His body stiffened slightly. As if my words had made him realize I was going to be fucking him. A man. I thought he was going to shove me off. Remember that he was not gay. That he wasn't interested in men. His eyes were ablaze with lust and heat. The emotion seeping out of him felt fucking good. The man felt everything more than anyone I'd ever met. I consumed those emotions like a starving man, fueling me. At this rate, I'd fucking summon some natural disaster that'd destroy this world.

Then something shifted. Pleasure turned to a frenzied lust. An imbalance of power. Eric twisted his body and threw me on my back, his body over mine, thrusting his hips against me. The role reversal was something I'd never allowed to happen before. I never bottomed. I was the one that did the fucking. Always.

He leaned in to kiss me, but I turned my head. "No," I breathed out. "Not on the mouth."

That seemed to piss him off. "So I'm good enough to fuck but not kiss?"

I wanted to tell him it wasn't that. Kissing was something too intimate for me. I couldn't give him that much power over me, but he took our cocks in his hand and resumed where I left off and my words turned into moans of pleasure. He collected the precum from my blunt head on his fingers and drew a line from under my balls to the crack of my ass and rimmed my hole. I inhaled sharply. All words I'd meant to say forgotten as his fingers glazed over my entrance.

"Well, guess what, *Thomas*," he said. I bristled at the name. "How about if I fuck you instead?"

Fuck, yes, please. But I couldn't get the words out. After a millennium, I was still a virgin. I'd never allowed anyone to make me that vulnerable before. I wasn't even sure why I let Eric take control. The scent of him, the emotions pulsing out of him in waves of pleasure and pain, had me already hard and panting. Eric taking control was the hottest fucking thing in the universe. I wasn't going to keep him from doing what he wanted to me. From sating his need.

He grabbed the lube from his side table and squeezed a good amount into his fingers. "Relax," he whispered kindly. Cold fingers breached my entrance.

The burning sensation made me clench. "Relax, sunshine," he said. "Let me in."

The thought of him joining our bodies took over any misgivings I may have had. I wanted to feel him inside of me. So I forced myself to relax. To trust him. He pushed his finger inside of me and I lifted my hips, deepening the intrusion. Then a second finger breached my walls of muscle as he prepared me. It only took one more deep push to have my nerve endings firing, and a sense of fullness overcame me. I regretted not taking that kiss because now the sounds coming out of my throat were pathetic mewling for more. A desperate cry for him to take all of me, and fast. For a straight guy, he knew what the fuck he was doing. Then I remembered he wrote fucking porn. The guy must know more shit than me. His practice was pretty fucking spot on, which made me growl thinking of him with someone else.

He chuckled. "You're growling."

I reined in the thoughts.

He released me and climbed off the bed. I thought he'd changed his mind. He was going to leave my ass wanting.

"Roll over," he ordered.

Without giving it much thought, I did. Like a submissive. I'd never submitted myself to anyone. Exposing my back and ass to him was a risk. I may have been older than hell, but I wasn't immortal in the traditional sense. Death was not an impossibility. This vessel could die, and I'd be reborn again. But that would leave my brothers vulnerable until I came of age. The reason I trusted no one. The reason I'd never exposed my back to anyone.

Until now.

Chapter Ten

Eric

What am I doing? As I watched Thomas turn over, my first instinct was to run. Far away. Get away from him. Now. While he was vulnerable. The thought both unnerved me and made me horny as hell. I was tired of being controlled. I wasn't going to be controlled in my own house, in my own bedroom. This was where I drew the line. He wanted me. Well, he'd have to do it my way.

I didn't think he would.

But he did.

And, oh shit, my cock felt painful and ready to slide into his ass cheeks and find that pretty hole of his. I had no clue what I was doing. Everything I'd learned about sex came from books and maybe some porn. All in the name of research. This was different. This wasn't in theory anymore. This was real. I didn't want to consider the ramifications of my actions right now. I just wanted to feel something other than pain.

I rubbed my erection along the crease of his ass for a few strokes. "You like that?"

He said something into the pillow I took as yes.

I pulled out, slid on the condom, and lubed myself, pausing with my cock at his entrance. "Is this what you want?" I asked, parting the globes of his ass and pushing deeper. "Tell me what you want me to do."

The sounds that came out of his throat were intoxicating. I wanted to give him everything he asked for. To give him this.

"Fuck me," he growled out.

Already open and gleaming with lube, his asshole pulsed. I tilted my hips, inching my cock inside in slow pulses, breaching the ring of muscle. He felt so damn tight and I considered taking him bare, wanted to feel the heat of him around my shaft.

Safety first, the condom stayed on. "Like this?" I breathed out. The heat of his body under me, the feel of his skin on my fingertips, and watching his hole swallow my cock as I bottomed out to my balls made me hypersensitive to the feel of him. That's when he started to moan. The man was loud in voicing his pleasure. Words like "More. Please. Fuck. Harder. Faster." were a jumbled mess that had me almost stroking out. Sweat dripped down my body as I tensed with the force of it. Of him. The desire and lust mounting. Skin slapping against skin. In and out, savoring the noises coming out of him along with the sound of wet suction between our bodies.

I hit his sweet spot and he cried out my name. The most beautiful sound in the world.

The desperate sound drew something out of me too, and I continued to thrust, impaling him. Right before orgasm, he clenched his ass around my cock. His body shook under me as he let out a sound that had every cell in my body rise to attention. A sound of pleasure that made me tingle all over. I did that for him. Me. His body continued to jerk as I ran my hand along his spine, feeling the hard muscles of his back as I chased my own release. I'd die if I didn't. And I knew I only had this one night. Just after his orgasm racked through his body, my body tensed, my balls tightened, and I spilled into the condom. I continued to jerk inside of him, riding the wave until I finally dropped onto his back. His scent of musk, sweat, and something I couldn't quite put my finger on enveloped me. It smelled like peppermint. I licked at his pulse point, tasting his sweat. Tasting *him* before my body went boneless.

"Fuck," he said, bringing me back to reality.

Fuck was the right word, all right. I couldn't find anything to say. I pulled out of him and fell on my back. He remained on his stomach, face turned away from me. I knew this was just some one-night fuck for him. I knew he'd somehow planned all this, and I had fallen into it. For whatever reason, he had wanted me and now he'd leave. I'd never see him again and that hurt. I'd never had a one-night stand before. Not with a woman or a man.

A man. I'd have to examine that hidden part of me later.

I got out of bed, pulled out the condom, and tied it before tossing it in the trash. Then I returned with a cool wet towel and aloe. With his face still turned away from me, I spread his ass cheeks and dabbed his entrance with the towel to ease whatever I'd done to him. Then I gently rubbed aloe on his hole. He moaned in pleasure but still didn't turn to look at me.

I didn't bother to shower. Instead, I regathered the covers and slipped beside him, giving him my back. A few long moments later, he sidled next to me, spooning me again. His body was so damn warm it made me shiver. I felt his breath on top of my head, his hand over me. Our fingers laced together. His were so soft. Mine, coarse. Different. His complexion pale compared to my darker coloring. To think that I'd just met him and had him in my bed.

Him.

I wasn't as freaked out as I probably should've been.

Something told me he wouldn't be staying for breakfast. That he wouldn't take me out on a proper date or hold my hand as we walked down Main Street. I wouldn't wake up nuzzled in his embrace again or meet his family and he wouldn't meet mine—which wasn't a bad thing. I wouldn't spend holidays with him or vacations in Rome or Cozumel or some cheesy vacation spot where we could form memories to cherish. I wouldn't learn his favorite food or dessert. I would never know which side of the bed he liked to sleep on or how his mouth felt on my body. We wouldn't grow old together.

"What are you thinking about right now?" he asked as his lips brushed my ear, sending all sorts of heat shooting down my body. I couldn't tell him the truth, so I settled for curiosity.

"Did you wake up this morning hell-bent on getting me into bed?" I wasn't sure if I meant that as a bad joke.

"Yes," he said, tickling my ear with his lips. "And I always get what I want."

I shivered. "Why me?"

He didn't answer, as if the silence negated the lie. "Fine, keep your secrets," I snapped.

In a gentle but swift movement, he turned me onto

my back to look at him. I was trapped in his embrace. The feel of his body against mine drew out more need for him. I wondered if he'd at least let me feel his mouth on mine.

"I didn't intend for it to get this far."

"It?" I bristled this time. After being alone for so long, I had been craving intimacy. And despite *it* just being sex for him, it was intimate for me. It meant so much more than words could ever convey. "You know what? Forget it."

I started to get up, but he pushed me back onto the bed. He straddled me, both hands on either side of my head, his hard body pressing down on mine. Blood rushed to my cock, making it throb against the underside of his balls. I hated my body's response to him. It shouldn't have happened. None of this was real. I'd been horny for the past five years. The only reason my body was responsive to his touches. It wasn't because of him. It could've been anyone. Anyone but Sheriff Swanky.

"It was perfect," he said.

"Then kiss me," I challenged. Unsure why.

His blue eyes roamed over my face, searching for something I couldn't name. "You said you'd give me anything within your power, do you remember that?" he said, sliding against my body so our cocks were slotted again. Grinding us. The friction sent jitters running through me and I bit my bottom lip to keep from moaning out. The sensation was delicious. I didn't want him to stop.

"I didn't say that." I breathed in an inhale of pleasure.

"You said whatever I need that you could provide

is mine for the taking."

Yes. I did say that. He brushed his lips against my jaw, down my neck. "I'm not giving you my firstborn," I said.

He pulled away from my body and, instantly, cold swept through me. The gap between us was too wide. I wanted him back against me but didn't dare reach for him. "I don't want your sons. But I will have your body." With a nefarious gleam in his eyes, he slowly dragged his lips down my chest, my stomach, and lower. Then he licked me from base to tip, swiping the precum from the head of my dick. I instinctively tilted my hips, chasing the warmth of his mouth. "Patience, baby," he said.

Damn, I wanted to taste myself on those full lips gleaming with my juices. The want so damn strong that it felt like ice cold water on my heated skin jolting me back to reality. The reality in which I wasn't made for just pleasure. The reality where things like this didn't happen to me. My comfort zone totally shredded. The many emotions sluicing through me too painful to pick apart. I couldn't do this. I needed him to leave. The sooner the better. To get out of my bed, my cabin, my life. He was leaving anyway.

I shoved him back hard and got to my feet in a fit of panic. He was strong enough to force me back onto my back and do whatever the hell he wanted to do with me. His expression turned sour, as if he didn't want to deal with my shit right now. Well, good for him. I didn't want him to deal with my shit right now. "You should leave," I said, panic settling its ugly grip tighter.

"Are you throwing me out?" He got out of bed like a predator, approaching me as if he were about to devour me.

"Yes," I stammered. My dignity flew out the window. I stepped away until my back hit the wall, and he was almost on my toes, hovering over me. His expression hardened, and eyes darkened. The playfulness and teasing gone. In its place stood a very dangerous man who exuded all kinds of possessiveness and power I couldn't wrap my mind around. This man could snap my neck. He could carry me over his shoulder and take me somewhere very unpleasant. Except I didn't feel threatened by him. I didn't believe he would hurt me. Instead, I felt his pain, his confusion, and his fears. They were all-consuming and almost dropped me to my knees.

"Don't dismiss me so easily, my *chosen*." He drew his finger along my temple, down my face, to my jaw line, and lifted my chin. His eyes hungrily lowered to my lips, and I gave a sharp inhalation of breath.

I wanted the kiss. I desperately wanted *his* kiss.

He slowly narrowed the gap between us, placing his other hand on the back of my head as if he thought I'd pull away. Not happening. I ached to feel his lips on mine, to savor and taste him on my tongue. He brushed his lips gently against mine, inhaling me as he went, savoring every second of me. The hottest thing I'd ever experienced in my life. His tongue gently slid along my bottom lip. Too eager, too afraid, too compromised to touch him, I remained still. Giving him back control. Slowly, he lifted his eyes to mine. A sharper blue. A blue that made me hold my breath. A blue I'd never seen before in nature or otherwise. Then he pressed his lips against mine. A decadent pleasure I so desperately wanted. No, *needed*.

Then the window beside us exploded.

Shards of glass flew inside. The force of the gale that followed tossed us onto our backs near the bed. Thomas wrapped his arms protectively around me. His body landed over mine, cradling my head. Protecting me.

"Oh, God, are you okay?" I managed to say after my senses returned.

He nodded but the fury in his expression spoke volumes on how the night had turned into one hot mess after another. "Are you hurt?"

"No, I—I don't think so." Though it was hard to breathe, I was pretty sure it had little to do with the fact that my window just imploded and more to do with this man on top of me.

Chapter Eleven

Zane

After we dressed and cleaned up the mess in the bedroom, we headed to the living room. The bedroom now tainted. While Eric plopped himself on the sofa, I headed to the kitchen. The whole night was a total fucking disaster. The window bursting the icing on the damn cake.

"Don't dismiss me so easily, my chosen."

My chosen.

The words had spilled out of my lips with no thought, and it felt so fucken right. Eric was mine. *Mine.*

I opened and slammed the cabinets shut, searching for a fucking drink. My hands shook. Every movement had me scenting him, yearning to enfold him in my arms and take him to pleasures he'd only imagined. It made me seethe with rage. I couldn't have him. I was too volatile and he was too hypersensitive. Feeding me his emotional distress. He simply felt too much and too deep. I'd been drawn to that part of him when we first met and had latched on to his emotional range like a fucking newborn to his mother's tit.

Fuck. I wanted to roar.

"Lower left corner," Eric said from where he sat staring at the fireplace where Boomer had died just a few hours ago. His world shattered. And I had taken advantage of his vulnerability. No sugar-coating that truth.

Did I regret it? No. Hell no.

Did he? Probably. Who was I kidding? Yeah. He regretted it.

I pulled out the bottle of Grey Goose and filled two glasses. I handed Eric one and then took a seat in the one armchair across the sofa not trusting myself to sit next to him. Holding back the need to toss him over my shoulder and carry him away with me.

The window shattering had been no accident.

And it saved me from making the biggest mistake of my life. The booze helped calm my nerves, but I'd need more than booze to calm my soul. Eric ran his palms on his thighs nervously. His hair was a mess of curls, his eyes wide and aware, gnawing his lower lip. The sex we'd just had tainted. I wondered what he thought about it all. What he thought about me. And why the fuck I cared so damn much.

The memories of the night I met Eric played in my head. I'd been meeting a client at a restaurant in Chicago. The dead of winter, the night had been cold. A thick layer of snow on the ground. I hated the cold. And snow.

"It's over, Eric."

The woman's voice drew my attention to a couple at the next table. I could only see the back of the man's head. "Layla, please. Let's just talk about this." The sound of his voice felt like daggers sliding into my soul.

"We have talked, and nothing is going to change. We are done. Just sign the divorce papers and move on with your life." The woman stormed off.

Eric had paid the check, taking his time to leave. Although I sensed the pain and heartbreak, I also felt a darker void inside of him. A shattered hopelessness. The same thing I'd sensed in Marie, right after I'd told her I wasn't going to mate her. She'd driven into a tree and killed herself that same night. He'd kept his head down as he left the restaurant, and I had followed him out.

Working on instinct, I reached him just as he opened the driver's door and tore the keys out of his hands. Then I shoved him into the passenger side and climbed in, taking off before he could even figure out that I was kidnapping him. Sobbing, he clung to the door staying as far away from me as he could.

"I'm not going to hurt you."

He chuckled. A phlegmy sound coming from his stuffed nose. "Says the man who kidnapped me. How do I know you're not some sort of serial killer?"

"Good point. I guess you're going to have to trust me."

He snorted.

"You're in no condition to drive. Where do you want me to take you?"

"I don't care," he mumbled.

I'd taken him to a cheap motel where he checked himself in. I should've left him then, but I couldn't. The night, dark and cold. He had left the door open, as if knowing I'd follow. We had spent that night clothed, in bed, in each other's arms. I had left before dawn.

And leaving him hadn't been easy then, just like it wasn't easy now.

Eric lifted sad eyes to me. Those brown eyes that pulled at everything that made me want to be enough

for him. The drink in his hand. "How could this have happened?" he asked.

I wasn't sure if he meant the window, or us. I went with explaining the window. "The snowstorm is pretty strong. It must've been the wind." Humans tended to clutch onto rationality even when there was no rational explanation. Eric nodded though I was sure once his head cleared, he'd probably come to a different conclusion.

"Are you leaving?"

Every knotted emotion in my body warred for release. "Yes. Bennett will be here in a few minutes."

He didn't look away from me. "Will I ever see you again?"

A silent roar passed through me. If Bennett didn't arrive soon, I would take Eric in every way possible. I'd mate him, bind him to me, and make him mine for all eternity. I needed to get the fuck out. "No," I grounded out through clenched teeth. Because if I ever saw Eric again, I would make him mine. And nothing would fucking stop me.

"We've met before," he said, making me stiffen, almost hopeful. Pushing everything else into the deep pit behind my heart. "You sound familiar."

"Yes, we've met."

The space between his brow folded as he tried to remember. But Eric hadn't really looked at me that night. He'd kept his eyes away and had cried until his eyes were swollen. Admitting that it was me that night would lead to nothing good. So I lied. "It was at a book signing event. Random."

"You read romance?" A hint of a smile warmed his features. Brought him back to a pleasant headspace,

forgetting the window for a moment.

"My brother. I was there with him."

He sipped his drink and gently put the glass on the table. Headlights pierced through the cabin windows announcing my retreat. I achingly got to my feet, ignoring the centuries of instinct that would've had me claiming what belonged to me. Eyes like warm honey latched onto mine as I approached him. I didn't want to sense regret, but it was there in bright neon. He closed his eyes as I swept my fingers across his forehead, down his cheek. "Sleep, Eric." My voice filled with a power he couldn't fight, lulling him to sleep. "Nothing will ever hurt you. I promise you that." Pliant under my touch, I gently guided him to lay down on the sofa and covered him with a blanket.

"It's okay," he whispered, eyes closed. "I'm going to be okay."

I wasn't going to be okay. That was the problem.

I watched him for a few minutes, absorbing the peacefulness of his sleep. This shouldn't have happened. I should never have come here because the moment I'd seen him again I knew I'd need more than one night. Outside, the bitter wind bit at my exposed skin, forcing me to shiver.

I hated the cold.

Chapter Twelve

Eric

"You are not traveling over two thousand miles to bury my dog," I told my youngest son, Sebastian, on the phone.

I'd woken up alone and cold. Having, for one brief moment, someone to share your bed with right before it was snatched away made the emptiness more palpable. Thomas had made me realize how alone I'd been these past eighteen months. Before then, I'd been busy being a father to my boys. Sebastian's entry into college had been hard for both of us, considering he'd been the one to find me unconscious and half dead. The one weakened moment in my life that I regretted more than anything. I wish I could turn back time and wipe that memory from him, give him a clean slate, and not the image of his father's failed suicide attempt.

"I'm fine, Sebastian. Really. Rosa and Trudy will be with me."

Sebastian snorted. "Then I really should be with you, Dad. Those two together are like fire and ice."

My son was very perceptive. Reminded me of me. "You may be right, but I'm still not letting you miss school to hold my hand. I'm fine, son. Really." I hope I sounded convincing. Although I felt better, there was nothing but emptiness inside. I suspected it had something to do with the man who had left me on the sofa early this morning. I still had no clue how my window had shattered, either. The wind hadn't attacked any other cabins in the area but mine.

Stranger than fiction.

"Maybe I should quit school," Sebastian whispered so low I almost missed the words.

My body instantly grew cold. I wanted nothing more than to revert to the dad I'd been when my kids were younger. They were always encouraged to pursue what they excelled at. I urged them to do something meaningful with their lives—not to be me. But as adults, this had to be their decision, and I'd always known Sebastian wasn't as receptive to change as Alejandro. Like me, Sebastian needed more time to acclimate. He felt things exponentially. I couldn't be a hypocrite and not address the big fat elephant in the room. Sebastian had that trait from me.

"Why?" I asked instead. "If you think I'm at risk—"

"No, Dad," he said quickly. "It's not that."

I sensed he was lying. Or at least not telling the whole truth. "Then what is it?"

"I just don't know what to study. I don't know what I want to be when I grow up."

I chuckled. "Well, luckily for you, you can be a career student until you figure it out. I have more than enough money."

"I know," he said coolly. "Because you live in hovels and the backcountry. You hoard your money the way Mom hoards her shoes."

Ouch.

"I don't need money."

"You earned it, Dad. What are you running from?

Me? Alejandro?"

I pressed my fingertips against the bridge of my nose, closing my eyes. "No. You know I'm not. You're the reason—" I couldn't finish the thought. He was literally the reason I was still alive.

"I know. I was there. I don't want to be here. I don't belong here."

Fuck. "Okay, fine. Just finish this year. I'll be there for Alejandro's graduation, and then we'll figure things out together. Okay?"

There was an edge of silence and then he consented.

"I love you," I said.

"Love you too," he said right before he hung up.

I tossed my phone on the bed. The bed I'd yet to clean of Thomas's scent. I'd kept the two versions of the man separate in my head. The one who had been kind and helped me with Boomer, and the one who had left me the night after. It was the only way I could sort through my muddled emotions.

Later that day, I had picked up Boomer's ashes. With Rosa's and Trudy's help, we buried her at the base of her favorite oak tree at the edge of the property. By the time I got home, old man Rueben had replaced the busted window in my room. I still had lingering thoughts about how that window had exploded just as Thomas was about to kiss me. As if a big warning sign had stopped us.

Yeah. My imagination working overtime.

With Rosa's help, I had done some digging into Thomas Raine. He had paid cash at the fundraiser and had checked into his hotel room as Thomas Raine. Rosa even contacted a friend at one of the private hangars and there was nothing on him or Bennett. So either he didn't leave via plane or he used a different name. Mrs. Owens hadn't been much help, either. Except for a New York home address that ended up being a high-end restaurant, she had nothing. That's as far as my search went. The guy didn't want to be found, so I stopped looking.

Four months later, I locked up the cabin, donated what didn't fit in my duffle, and headed to LA to watch my older son graduate college and try to convince my younger son to stay in college. Before I left, Rosa had made me promise to keep in touch and, as my life coach, I expected to.

LA was exactly what I expected for an early June afternoon. Scorching hot and cloudy. After being in a small town, I realized I disliked big city life. The traffic and the crowds frazzled my nerves. All I wanted was to slip between the sheets on a bed and close my eyes against the chaotic world. Instead, I headed to the pavilion, where Alejandro would graduate with his mother and brother beside him.

He'd had a choice of two people to walk with him during this most momentous occasion, and he had chosen his mother and brother. I can't say it hadn't stung when Sebastian had told me. Because Alejandro couldn't tell me himself. As always, I shoved all the hurt and pain aside and acted as if it made sense. Sure, his mother had abandoned us when he was sixteen, while I tried my best to survive the loss. I wasn't a perfect parent, but at least I was there.

Yeah, asshole. Until you tried not to be, remember?

Guilt and blame were something I carried around like a shield against the rest of the world. A reminder of everything I didn't deserve. The reason I cried alone that night after Sebastian told me. Alejandro had every right to hate me. I was so proud of him and would always be proud of him.

So with a wide smile planted on my face, I watched proudly as he walked the stage with his mom and brother, while I snapped a gazillion photos. Afterward, I met them at a sandwich shop next to UCLA's campus. Sebastian stood waiting for me outside despite that he had given me his exact coordinates. I realized when I saw his thick black hair and kind brown eyes, how much I missed him these past few months. I drew him into a hug, and while Alejandro would've admonished me for the public display of affection, Sebastian melted into the hug. The kid was a hugger.

"I missed you," I whispered.

I felt him shiver slightly, but he didn't say anything. "Come on, we already ordered."

I followed him to Alejandro who was already digging into his burger with his mouth full. He fist-bumped me in greeting.

I sat where Sebastian had placed my food. "I ordered for you. I hope it's okay."

"Of course it is."

I caught Alejandro giving him an eye roll.

Instinctively, I ran my hand along my neck. Thankfully, Sebastian had turned away from me. Only Alejandro caught my gesture and practically sneered at me. I quickly lowered my hand onto the table. "So," I started, easing into the conversation. "What's the plan this summer?"

Alejandro went on to inform me that the job he got lined up at Wolfe Technologies in New York was still a green light. He'd been working his ass off for it and I was so proud of him. Unlike me, Alejandro was a mover and shaker. I turned to Sebastian. "What about you?" I knew Sebastian had made plans early in the semester to volunteer with his sociology class and head to Brazil to help build homes. "What's the plan?"

He shrugged but didn't look at me. His long, thick hair hid his face.

"What happened to Brazil?"

"I pulled my application. I changed my mind."

Alejandro snorted. Sebastian lifted his eyes in derision and kicked his brother under the table, not even trying to hide it. Something they always did when they were angry at each other. Usually, it was Alejandro hiding something from me, not Sebastian.

"What is it?"

"I figured I'd stay with you, like you said, to figure things out together."

"For the summer," I clarified.

"Yeah."

Alejandro snorted again, and once more received a swift kick for the response. "Tell him. He's going to find out anyway."

"Like he's going to find out about Cammie being pregnant?" That got Sebastian a kick from his brother.

"Okay, time out," I said, gesturing a T with my hands. "What is this about a pregnancy? You are using condoms, right?"A few people shot a look our way, but I was beyond caring.

"Dad," Alejandro said, looking like a tomato, "lower your voice. Yes. I use protection."

"Then what is this about this girl?"

"If she is, it's not mine."

Ohmygod, I wanted to throttle this kid. At least he superseded me in the whole marriage department. By the time I was his age, I had a two-year-old and one on the way. I turned to Sebastian, who I knew needed a bit more delicacy than his brother. "What's going on?"

"I hate it here. You said to finish the year. I finished the year."

I felt my blood drain. "What did you do?"

He didn't respond. Alejandro did. "He dropped out."

I couldn't stifle my disappointment.

"Mind your business, dick."

"I try but you make it hard, klinger."

A couple of more kicks under the table had them both wincing before they finally settled.

"I want to stay with you," Sebastian said. Poor kid looked like a tormented soul—like looking in a mirror.

"Of course you can stay with me. But that doesn't give you a free pass to do nothing. Work, school, or the military. Those have always been the three options."

"I'll work."

"Doing what? Cleaning toilets?" Alejandro said dryly.

Thankfully, Sebastian didn't try to kick him. "I'll figure it out."

I had to give it a moment as we ate in silence. Was there anything I could say to change Sebastian's mind? College would be a good experience for him. I wanted him to have the things I didn't have growing up. Choices. College had been a pipe dream for me. Too expensive and too challenging with my below-average grades. The reason it'd been so easy just to settle down and conform. I didn't want that for my kids. They deserved better. But they had to make that choice for themselves.

"So that means I have to get a two-bedroom. Any preferences?"

Alejandro shifted in his seat. I knew he was bothered by it all. Despite his carefree attitude, Alejandro protected his brother fiercely, even from me. Then he lifted his eyes staring behind me with an awkward smile on his face. Even before I turned to look at who he was smiling at, I already knew. I'd seen her from afar on the stage with Alejandro a few hours ago. She had worn a flowy dress that didn't highlight the curves I knew so well. I hadn't seen her up close since Sebastian's high school graduation. The year I sold the house and moved away.

Every time I saw her, it felt as if she were ripping out the gauze I'd put around my heart to stop the bleeding.

"Sorry," Sebastian whispered. "We told her to wait until you left."

I appreciated that sentiment, but Layla Ortega wasn't someone who took orders very well. My windpipe felt constricted, and if I didn't unclog whatever had been buried inside of me, I was going to pass out. It'd never get better. Ever.

She didn't look at me right away as the boys got to their feet and hugged her. Then she took the seat on my other side before she finally met my eyes. Those hazel green eyes plucked at all my imperfections. Warm blonde curls framed her face. As always, she looked beautiful. Except that she didn't quite fit at the table and had to push her chair back. It's when I noticed her swollen baby bump.

Baby.

Layla was pregnant.

At forty-two!

Why? She was too old. She could have complications. The baby could be born with health problems. Any number of things could happen. I wanted to scold her for being careless, like Alejandro, but my words wouldn't pass. Especially when she leaned forward and sifted her delicate fingers into my beard. I had left it untamed since Thomas left me.

"This is new," she said with a sultry smile.

I had to remember that Layla wasn't making a pass at me with that touch or smile. That it was just my imagination. That my fool heart wanted to believe that every touch, every look meant something more when it didn't. I pulled back. "Yeah." That one word response seemed to piss her off because she scowled, folded her hands neatly on the table, and turned her focus to Sebastian, who squirmed beside me. At nineteen, and taller than both of us, the sight seemed wrong. "Alejandro, can you wait for me with Pedro? He's in the Mercedes."

As if I cared what car her new husband drove.

Alejandro quickly retreated without so much as a glance my way. I took in his appearance. Wearing a tee-shirt and jeans, Alejandro had always been athletic. He looked much older than his twenty-two years, and I wanted to hold this image of him in my heart before he left to live his own life.

"I'm assuming he's told you about dropping out," Layla started without preamble.

"It's not dropping out. I finished the year. I'm just taking a break."

"You can't take a break from life, Sebastian."

"I'm not. I'm going to work."

She huffed and turned to me with a lifted brow. "Aren't *you* going to say something?"

I hated when she held that condescending tone with me. As if I were her child. Although I did agree with her, I wasn't going to push Sebastian away. Not when he clearly needed guidance. "I think we have the summer to figure things out," I said. "We'll take it day by day."

Layla made a sound like a snort-growl. She was good with those. "Of course you would. You plan nothing. Hell, this is your fault."

"Mom," Sebastian hissed out.

But Layla was on a roll, and I couldn't do anything but take it because she was right. "If it hadn't been for what you did, for what you tried to do—"

"Mom! Stop it!" Sebastian jumped to his feet.

Layla glowered at him. "Don't make me out to be the bad one. I'm not the one that almost killed myself and made you watch."

"That's enough." Sebastian grew taller, if that was possible. "This is my decision and has nothing to do with that, or him. This is about *me*."

Slowly, she got to her feet. "That's why I want you to stay with Pedro and me for the summer. I think we can work things out. You can try different things. Pedro knows people."

The guy was a fucking salesman. Talked shit and collected souls.

"No. I'm staying with Dad."

She looked at me. There was no doubt in my mind that she wanted me to tell him to stay with her. It might've been the best for his future, but I had the now to worry about. And Sebastian was old enough to make his own choices. I had to trust him in that.

"It's up to him," I said. "He's an adult."

"Yes, he is," she breathed out, rubbing her swollen belly. I wondered how long it would take after she had that kid before she forgot him altogether. "Fine, honey. Let's go, and I'll drop you off wherever you want later."

Sebastian turned to me as I got up from the chair. My bones felt heavy. I numbed out the sharp words she'd thrown at me. I deserved them. "I'll text you the address."

"Do you even have a place this time?"

I ignored Layla and hugged my son again. "I'll see you later."

He nodded and walked out without waiting for his mother. She turned to me with a much softer expression, as if she actually cared about me. "He deserves so much better," she whispered. "I hope you realize that."

I knew what she meant. He deserves to have Pedro as a father. He deserves anyone but me. I said nothing, and she went away like she always did.

I tossed our trash and walked under the bright June California sun.

Life could always get worse.

Chapter Thirteen

Zane

The malice's thick, inky black hair covered his face as he sat hunched over, his chin dipped onto his chest. Despite the two bullet wounds, fourteen stab wounds, and a cleaver splitting the two hemispheres of his brain, the thing still breathed. Our people have been at war with the malice for thousands of years. They were mimics with the ability to blend into human society. They had all the biological make-up to pass perfectly— two hundred and six bones, seventy-eight organs, including a heart, brain, liver, lungs, and genitals. Except, instead of a human soul, their core consisted of darkness. Instead of human emotions, they possessed no sympathy, no fear, no joy, only purpose. And their purpose was to help bring about the end of the world.

They had one flaw in their design. They had to adhere to the limitations of their biology. They were, for all intents and purposes, human. They had a nervous system and felt pain. Like lust, pain I could consume. The demon inside me basked in it. It filled me with a euphoric power that had my nerve endings firing up with a rather pleasant sensation.

"If you start to jack off, I'm out of here," Xcian hissed out.

"It only happened once."

"You're disgusting," my brother said dryly.

"And you have yet to come into your own. I can give you a taste now, if you'd like."

"Fuck you," Xcian spit out.

As the second oldest, Xcian would inherit my powers should I kick the bucket and perish. The reason my brother was so hell-bent on being my personal bodyguard. The reason I hadn't put a knife through my own brain stem. I loved my brothers and would never want them to suffer what I had. I wouldn't tell him that, though. There was a certain satisfaction in riling up my successor.

Xcian dumped a bucket of cold water onto the malice's head, jolting it awake. Blood pooled at his feet and swirled down the drain. We took care of business at one of the numerous warehouses we owned throughout the city. No one would hear him scream. Although alive, his vessel was ruined. He wouldn't survive long. Not that I intended for him to survive longer than it took for him to give me the information I required. The fucker had killed two humans and I wanted to know why.

I grabbed the wet, inky hair and pulled back his head. Black eyes turned to human green in a second before a smirk cracked his features. "What is the plan this time?" I asked. "I'll make it swift, or we can be here all month." A flash of fear passed over his face, replaced by hatred. "Do you even know why you hate us so much?" In truth, *I'd* even forgotten what started the fight. "We can live together. Share resources. Has that ever occurred to you?"

The thing seemed to consider it for a moment. I knew this part. It was always the same. Had it been my father torturing him, Alastair Crawford would've continued the beating without attempting a truce. I had grown softer in my years of life. I always gave them a chance at redemption.

The thing spat at my suit.

They never took it.

"You and your kind are maggots. We'll stomp you with our boots and take over this realm."

"Why? Why kill two worthless maggots?"

A stream of blood ran down his lip as he smiled. A grotesque, inhuman look. "They were a means to breach your union."

I stiffened. Although we had anticipated threats during my engagement party, the malice admitting to it so blatantly meant they probably had what they needed to wreak havoc and chaos. To bring about bloodshed and war.

"Did you ever wonder why you have yet to secure a union?" The thing, no longer human, smiled.

My body coiled tight. My stomach knotted. Throughout the years, I'd been betrothed a total of seven times. All of them died before the union. Plague. A plane crash. A shooting. An earthquake. Drowning. A heart attack. The last one died when she'd lost control of her car and slammed into a tree. She died instantly. All of them died within weeks of the binding ritual. When they would be of my blood.

I shoved the knife under his chin.

Xcian said something I didn't catch.

"What do you mean?" I hissed out, driving the blade deeper and slicing his skin. "What the fuck are you saying?"

"Keep this one close or—" The guy's head

exploded.

I shut my eyes just in time to keep brain matter from blinding me. Chunks of scalp, eyeballs and shit covered my face and torso. I released him and cursed. "You fucking, son of...mother...asshole, prick!" I used the bottom of my shirt to wipe my face. I knew there was shit in my hair too. As he put the gun back into his holster, I cursed and glared at him. "Jesus, fucking Christ, Galen. I needed him to talk."

"The Furies required his end." My brother Galen carried the chthonic demons of vengeance. A pain-in-the-ass need to kill those who have broken a vow or taken a life. At this point, the Furies were making shit up as they went.

"He had no more information to give us," Hawke said. My brother, born after Galen. Too bad he wasn't the oldest. Hawke would've been a better heir. He stuck to rules and protocol like flies on shit. "He was rattling your fucking cage. *I* even felt it." Hawke strutted toward the dead thing that now didn't even resemble a human. He glared at Xcian. "And you shouldn't have let it get this far."

Xcian shrugged. The only one of the nine who possessed my mother's silver hair and eyes, Xcian also possessed a hint of her power of sight. "At least he's not masturbating."

I glowered at my brothers and shot Xcian a middle finger then started making circular movements as if indicating what I'd be doing to my asshole later.

"You're funny," he deadpanned.

Hawke, Galen, and Xcian went to work in hosing the fucker. One thing good about the malice was that they quickly rotted once they stopped pumping oxygen into their cells. As if the years had just caught up with them and all we had to do was flush them down the drain. Even their bones turned to ash. Made the cleanup easy with a pressure hose.

"Serena?" I asked my brother. The thought of them having anything to do with the deaths of my betrotheds felt too real.

"She's fine. With the twins."

I rolled my eyes. An anomaly that made us ten, and not nine. Basil and Sage came in a set and could drive the sanest person mad.

"She's not happy," I said.

Xcian snorted. "No shit. Sage will have anyone contemplating their sanity."

"She doesn't want to marry you," Hawke responded, ignoring Xcian's comment. "Just like you don't want to marry her." Hawke lowered the water pressure.

I started to undress so he could hose me down of the blood and goop.

"I don't know why you make this shit difficult," he admonished. Hawke never went against the House rules. Fucking annoying.

I wanted someone I could spend the rest of my life with who actually loved me. That was the difficult shit Hawke was talking about.

"It's not like you have to be faithful," Xcian added. "Just put a baby in her belly and do what you've been doing."

Hawke growled and shot Xcian with the hose, only he'd upped the pressure and Xcian fell on his ass. "Fucker," Xcian spat, and launched himself at Hawke. They both went sprawling onto the wet floor, wrestling.

Though they were both morons, if I had to bet on who would fold, it would be Hawke. Xcian's demon would never let him lose.

Beside me, Galen fisted his hands. I could feel the demons writhing inside of him at the display of violence. If Hawke and Xcian didn't stop, I wouldn't put it past Galen to kill them too.

"They're just horsing around," I said.

That seemed to calm Galen's demon. "I'm heading out. Call if you need me." With that, he walked out. Galen was third in line and if Xcian and I fucked up our inheritance, leaving Galen to hold it, the world *would* end. The Furies were just too damn insatiable with the need to pass vengeance, and nowadays everyone had something in their past and present to answer for.

"If you can't handle the truth," Xcian shot out to Hawke, "then you shouldn't fucking be around."

I pointed a warning finger at Xcian. "Stop provoking the shit."

He opened his mouth and then snapped it shut. At least *he* knew when to shut the fuck up.

The clean-up had been easier than facing my parents, but both incidents were equally messy. When we got home, with Hawk nursing a black eye, he and Xcian quickly made their rounds of greeting before disappearing into their rooms. The mansion was large enough that they could get lost for days without ever seeing anyone. Leander had been ten when that had happened, and mother had updated the archaic mansion with intercoms. I had found him curled up in one of the guest rooms, sensing his panic like a radar blip.

Mother was wearing a long, silver low-cut evening gown matching her long, silver hair. The fabric hugged her demure frame, making her look much, much younger than her two thousand years. Her silver eyes masked by green contacts filled with warmth when she saw me. For the past four months, I'd been too volatile to be in her presence. I didn't want her to sense neither my real issue nor my breaking heart. The adrenaline of the kill masked every other emotion swirling inside of me.

"Oh, honey, it's been too long. Your father is taking us to Genero's tonight."

I turned to my father. Except for my father's pale blue eyes, he and I were carbon copies of each other. Thick blond hair with pale streaks, deep-set eyes, thick brows, and a strong chin. We even had the same build.

"Do you think it a good idea to go out now? The malice—"

"I won't hide as if I'm afraid of those abominations," my father interrupted, forcing me to press my lips together. "You should know better." My father approached my mother and delicately took her hand, lifting it to kiss her palm. "I would never let anything happen to my family."

Unlike me. That snide remark said. I felt a pang of guilt shoot straight to my heart.

"You will be heir after your union," he said. "You better start acting like it." Father walked out of the room, leaving my mother to tend to me. As always.

She narrowed the gap between us and cupped my cheek. "He loves you, you know."

I had to restrain the need to roll my eyes. The parable of the prodigal son was a truth old as time. Irresponsible, reckless, ungrateful, spoiled—I had heard it all. Almost losing Leander had been my tipping point and Father would never let me forget it.

"I hope you found what you were looking for in Maine," Mother said.

I almost asked how she knew I'd gone to Maine but shouldn't have been surprised. My father would've tracked me the moment he allowed me to find some closure with my decision to bind myself with Serena. "I found nothing real." Though that was a lie. I'd found a man who I'd wanted to taste for more than one night. A man who'd, in just under twelve hours, made me laugh and cry and feel things I'd never thought I would ever feel. I craved his touch, his smile, his scent.

Mother watched me with her own sadness. "Love is but one emotion, my son. Undefinable in its radiance and within your grasp still."

I cupped her small hands in mine and kissed her palm. "Serena and I will make this work."

She sighed at my indifference. "I know you will do what is right."

The faith she placed in me hurt more than all the self-deprecating thoughts slamming through me. I wanted to do right by her, but I just didn't know how.

"Get ready. Sentinel will be meeting us at the club."

The last thing I wanted was to be around Serena after what the malice had admitted. I pushed the thought away and did as told. I was starting to get good at that.

Chapter Fourteen

Eric

I found myself cutting into a long line full of people half my age to sneak into a club bursting with music vibrating the floors and bodies clinging to each other under dark shadows. This was ridiculous. I would never find Alejandro in *that*.

"Come on," Sebastian said, and led me toward the large bouncer who stood at least six four with two hundred and something pounds of muscle and a look on his face that had all kinds of don't-mess-with-me vibes.

The guy gave Sebastian a slow, longing look from his dark thick hair down to his black boots that made me want to punch the man. Sebastian was still my baby boy and someone clearly eye-fucking him set me on edge. I thought I had left this side of me behind in high school. I hadn't fought since some asshole had started hitting on Layla in the tenth grade and wouldn't take no for an answer.

Sebastian whispered something to the giant of a man I didn't catch with all the vibrations and screaming coming from just inside the club. The man nodded and the rope came down, allowing us entrance. I grabbed Sebastian's arm just as we passed inside to stop him.

"What did you tell him?"

"I know him," Sebastian said. He didn't elaborate

which made me want to inquire more. Like how well did Sebastian know him? I wondered if I knew my own sons anymore. Sebastian had called to let me know Alejandro had gotten bad news from Cammie and he'd left his mother's party in a hurry. I'd followed Sebastian to where he thought his brother would hide out after life-changing news. A club had not been my first thought, hadn't even been anywhere near the first fifty places I'd thought Alejandro would go to contemplate being a father.

A father.

I wanted to strangle the kid.

"We're going to have to separate!" Sebastian yelled over the music. "It's the only way we have a chance at finding him."

I knew he was right, but I didn't want to separate. A growing need to protect Sebastian from predators in this place settled in my stomach. He was only nineteen, not even legal to be in here.

"Trust me, Dad," he said.

He worried about his brother. I was worried about his brother. I nodded and released the death grip I had on his arm. Sebastian disappeared among a sea of bodies on the dance floor as I headed toward the bar. I'd never liked clubs. It seemed like a place you'd go to have a one-night stand with someone. I'd fallen in love with Layla in high school. Shortly after, we were married with children. No need for clubs. I felt old. In my bones and in my heart. And my clock wound down at midnight, which had already passed.

I ordered a drink and caught sight of security cameras behind the bar. There was no way I could track down Alejandro in the place unless, maybe, through the security feed. It was worth a shot.

I'd seen enough movies to know that a good tip would go a long way to acquiring what I needed, which was access to the security area. I set a hundred-dollar bill on the bar, keeping my fingers on it. Alejandro would be paying me back for this one. The bartender, wearing pink lip-gloss and shimmering makeup that made him, well, shimmer, had sparkling blue eyes that sparkled when the beam of light hit them. The guy was breathtakingly beautiful. Just the thought made my stomach clench. My libido had certainly taken a turn outside my comfort zone. There was no such temptation when I'd remained in my small, neat cabin making up stories. LA was definitely different.

The guy leaned over, too close. Those sparkling blue eyes on me blew apart my thoughts until he lowered his eyes at the hundred in my hand. *Security camera. Alejandro.* My brain jolted back online. "Is there someone I can talk to about getting a visit to the security room?"

He lifted his eyes to the loft. "Owners up there, if you can get up there."

I handed him the hundred. "Thanks." He grabbed my hand, and I didn't know whether to pull away or lean in. I did neither.

"I got a thirty-minute break coming up." His eyes lowered to my lips. Definitely a flirtatious move making me wonder if I had my own neon sign on my face stating I was bi-curious. Was I bi-curious?

The guy slowly smirked just as I found my voice. "Okay," I said, unsure what else to say, and pulled away from him.

A set of security guards stood near the stairs up to

the loft. I expected them to stop me, but they just gave me a piercing gaze, nostrils flaring, then they looked away. I felt as if I'd just been vetted by a couple of hound dogs and released into the wild. Not wanting to question my luck, I took the steps two at a time. At the top step, I looked over the dance floor, searching for my missing sons. The place was huge. A narrow hallway led to the back of the club, where I figured the restrooms were. There were four bar areas and among the sea of dark hairs, I couldn't pick out anyone I recognized. I checked my phone but hadn't received a notification from either one of them.

I was so planning on grounding them both. I didn't care how old they were. Angry and worried, I stepped into the loft. Catching sight of a couple on the dance floor, it felt as though someone had slammed a bat against my chest.

I knew it was him even before he turned around.

I could never forget the soft, blond hair, or the broad expanse of his shoulders stretching the couture suit he wore. The last time I'd seen him, he'd been easing me into sleep on my sofa after my window exploded. Despite him leaving me, I had wanted to keep the memory of us alive. To hold it as something to revere. Something precious that I could keep. Except now *that* memory was tainted by this one. He was grinding against a beautiful, dark-haired woman as they danced on the private dance floor. Her back was to his chest, with one arm slung behind his neck. His hands were on her hips as she rubbed her ass against his crotch. His eyes hooded, his lips parted, I could feel the pleasure seeping from him as if he were caressing *me*. Then I let out the breath I didn't know I'd been holding, and he quickly jerked his head up, his eyes scanning the area but unable to see me.

"Can I help you?" a man with startling pale eyes and silver hair tied at the nape of his neck asked. "This is a private engagement party for the happy couple." He lifted his chin to Thomas and the woman. They had stopped dancing and grinding against each other and were now in deep conversation. The dark shadows made it hard to pick up any specific expressions. Her hand landed on his chest, and then she cupped his face.

"That's my brother, Zane, and his fiancée, Serena. Are you a friend?"

Zane. Not Thomas. Thomas had never existed. It was always Zane.

I felt sick. Thomas lifted his eyes, and I could've sworn he sensed me. He scanned the area, and a tiny part of me wished he were searching for me. That somehow, he knew I was here. That he'd have some sort of explanation for his lies. An explanation for using me, for turning me into something I'd never, *ever* wanted to be. The other. The lover. The home wrecker.

At that moment, I hated him. Pain struck smack in the middle of my chest where I had buried the agony of losing Layla, the love of my life. It forced me to stumble back. I was an idiot. A damn idiot. I turned away from the couple and almost slammed into Thomas's brother. I hadn't even realized he'd moved to block my path. The man had the lightest colored eyes I had ever seen. They almost looked colorless. He stood much taller than me, which didn't say much since I was average at five-nine. Built like a house, with long silver hair tied at the nape of his neck. His expression hardened when he looked at me and his nostrils flared as if catching a foul stench. He looked two seconds away from tossing me down the stairs.

"Sorry," I said. "Wrong turn." I started to leave when he took hold of my elbow. An electrical zap rushed through my skin, making me wince at the contact. He felt it too and quickly released me.

"Who are you?" he growled out.

"Nobody. I'm just leaving." *Please let me go.*

"Xcian!" Someone called, distracting the guy.

I took advantage of the interference and sprinted down the steps, through the bodies on the dance floor, trying to get to the exit. My nerves and body were out of whack thinking about Thomas. No, not Thomas. Zane. I got turned around. The ray of lights and shadows made it impossible to find a straight line to the exit. I ended up back at the bar. Unsettled and shaking from anger or shock or both, I grabbed onto the counter in a death grip. That's when I felt my phone buzz in my pocket.

A text from Sebastian.

—*Found Alejandro. Going to stay with him the night.*—

Exhaling a deep sigh, thoughts of murdering my eldest suddenly sounded good.

—*Okay. Will fight my way out of this place. You and Alejandro owe me big time. Grounded. For eternity.*—

Sebastian sent me a smiley emoji as if I were kidding. I wasn't.

"Everything okay?"

I looked up to see the handsome bartender smiling at me.

"Perfect," I said dryly. "You wouldn't happen to

have a shortcut out of here, do you?"

The smile on his face turned brighter. "I sure do. And a break."

After calling out that he was going on his break, he led me to the part of the bar that lifted, and to a back door. Five seconds later, I was breathing cool night air. I shuddered. The echo of pain remembering Thomas with his fiancée hollowed me out. Thomas had used me. No, not Thomas. Thomas didn't even exist. The lying cheat. Zane had hurt me. I suddenly wanted another memory to replace him. So when the guy shoved me against the wall and kissed me, I just went with it.

Chapter Fifteen

Zane

Seeing Riley's tongue down Eric's throat awoke the darkness I'd tried to keep at bay. It took everything I had not to rip off the guy's head from his shoulders. Thankfully, Xcian had followed me out and caught Riley as I pulled him off Eric.

My Eric.

Mine.

Eric's lips were moist and swollen from the kiss, inhaling a little gasp as Riley was torn from his arms.

"Oh, my God," Riley said. "Is he yours? I didn't know, Zane. Really, I didn't know."

I ignored the scowl on Eric's features. Seeing the fight in his eyes only edged me on, made me hard. The need for him awoke every cell in my body. I had let him go twice. Never again.

"Get him out of here," I ordered Xcian of Riley.

"It's okay, baby," Xcian reassured the young man. "No biggie. Just go back in and forget this happened."

Riley nodded and looked at Eric as if it'd be the last time he'd ever see Eric again. Damn straight it would. Once Riley disappeared back inside, I rounded on Eric to yell at him when a white-hot pain ignited on my left cheek, and I saw sparks of light behind my eyes. I'd just been slapped. Hard. My pride and the sound of my brother's gasp had hurt more. I'd never been slapped by anyone before. Not anyone who lived afterward, anyway.

The sheer angry expression on Eric's face had my gut twisted into knots. He lifted his other hand to slap me again when I shook off my stupidity and grabbed his wrist. Hard enough to stop the blow, but not hard enough to hurt him.

"Fuck you!" Eric spat.

I pinned his hands to his sides and leaned my body closer, one of my legs between his so he wouldn't try to unman me.

"Let me go, *Zane*," he ordered, writhing under me. The closeness of him had my body coiled tight and my cock harder than when I'd been with him last. "You liar. Let me go!"

"Relax," I said coolly. The last thing I wanted was to hurt him, but the evil inside me already started to circle closer to the surface. If he kept fighting me, it'd only be a matter of time before I turned him to face the wall, stripped his ass naked, and plunged deep into him.

"Go to hell, asshole. Or better yet, go back to your fiancée!"

Fuck. My heart took a tumble to my knees as his voice broke. His emotions were too damn strong to hide from me. "Let me explain."

"Explain? Explain that you made me into a home wrecker! Explain why you lied about leasing the cabin. Your name, *Thomas*! All of it was bullshit! Just some sick, twisted game you played to get me to fuck you. Well…well…go to hell!" He bucked his hips forward and used his body to slam into me. I stumbled back slightly but corrected my balance and shoved him back hard. This time, I cupped his throat and squeezed, biting back everything I wanted to say about meeting him five years ago. About how I could think of nothing but him during that time, driving me insane. I couldn't tell him I'd gone to that cabin to find a reason to breathe, and found something better. But I'd fucked it all up.

I couldn't tell him how I'd caught his scent in the club and almost lost my shit. How I would've killed Riley had Xcian not been there to take the kid away.

I couldn't tell Eric any of that because then it would make it real, and Eric deserved someone better than a monster.

The silence between us stretched for far too long. He had gone still, his breathing cool. I traced my thumb across the sensitive skin above his pulse. The compulsion to taste him, to breathe in part of his soul, was too strong to fight against. His lips parted on an inhale and I dipped into them. A few heartbeats away from joining us in breath, soul, and life. He stiffened under me and, just as I grazed his lips with mine, he turned his head away, unknowingly saving us both from the biggest mistake of my life.

"No," he said. "I'm not going to be the reason you hurt your fiancée."

I leaned my forehead against his temple. "I'm so fucking sorry, Eric."

He shook his head just as his eyes shut tight. "Just let me go."

Never. Eric was *mine*. "That's the thing," I said. "I can't." I brushed my lips against his ear and whispered the words that would set him to sleep. His legs crumpled, and I lifted him over my shoulder.

"You have lost your fucking mind," Xcian said.

My brother hadn't left me alone, had witnessed all of it.

I *had* lost my mind. No point in arguing that.

"You'd rather put a target on his head than let him go. Is that how you treat the people you care about?"

I spun to him with a growl. Eric's weight on my shoulder didn't allow me to swing my fists at the fucker. "It's not your fucking business. Stay out of it."

"Really?" he hissed. "You think I can stay out of your shit?"

My fuck-up meant that Xcian would be next in line to carry my pains and I had promised myself a long time ago that I wouldn't do that to him. I couldn't let him go through the shit I'd gone through because of my own selfishness. None of this was fucking right. "I've imprinted on him. He wears my scent."

Xcian's pale eyes turned hard, like looking at a soulless deviant. He ran his hand through his hair, releasing it from the leather tie. Silvery hair tumbled around his shoulders in strands like spun silk. Xcian had gotten our mother's features and some of her powers, although he denied it tooth and nail. "I know. I scented him when he saw you and Serena in the loft."

I narrowed my eyes at him. "And you let him go."

"He ran. I didn't follow. There's a difference."

I wrestled with the thought of strangling him despite a part of me knowing he was right. But there was no way to erase Eric from my soul. If shit went sideways with me, Xcian would be next in line to take my place. And he knew what it all meant, though I had kept the worst of it from him. "I'll figure this out. I just need him safe until after the union."

"You're still going to try to bind yourself to Serena?"

"I have no choice." It felt like shards of glass had dug into my heart. "I'll make this right, brother."

Bennett arrived shortly after with the car and Xcian helped me load Eric inside.

"He has two sons who will be looking for him. Can you keep an eye on them? Just make sure they are safe." I gave him Eric's wallet so Aristotle, the youngest, could do his computer thing and find the brothers.

"And Sentinel?" Xcian asked.

The archon was here to help me strengthen the prison I created inside the aether to keep the captured demons from breaking out. Until I shared my powers with an heir, the demons I'd trapped in the aether would become stronger. The evil, a part of my every breath. "Tell Mother I'll be back to speak with him."

"She's going to be pissed."

"I know."

Xcian sighed. "On my word," he said, fisting his chest over his heart in a vow.

I climbed into the front seat. Bennett didn't look too thrilled but knew better than to say anything. I was not in the fucking mood for a lecture.

Chapter Sixteen

Eric

I hadn't had a hangover from hell since my twenty-first birthday when my cousin Gerry had the bright idea of taking me to a strip club with a group of family and friends. I had passed out in the coatroom. It took them the entire night to find me. I'd never lived that one down. This hangover felt worse. I didn't even remember drinking that much.

Wait a minute. I didn't even remember drinking, period.

I remembered Sebastian, and also looking for Alejandro. Then...then Zane.

I passed out while arguing with him. He had whispered something to me before my legs crumpled and I had zoned out. He'd drugged me. The fucker had drugged me. With a groan, I managed to get to my feet. The world shifted under me for a heartbeat. I was going to be sick.

"It'll pass." Zane sat under shadows like some sort of creep, or stalker.

I needed to get my wits attached to my balls before I started crying. "Where am I?" My voice was dry and cracked.

He smoothly got to his feet without a sound as if he were a ghost. Too dark, I couldn't even see his face, only the outline of his large body until he was practically on me. My feet faltered, and he reached out to steady me. "Don't," I snapped.

He let out a soft sigh. "Then sit, before you fall and hurt yourself."

I dropped onto the bed unceremoniously. He walked to a separate room and turned on the lights. A bathroom. I heard the sink turn on, and then he returned with a small paper cup of water. "Drink."

I wasn't a dog to be ordered around. I would've told him to shove it, but my throat was too dry, so I took the offered water and drank all of it. "Kidnapping is against the law," I shot out as if he didn't know.

"There are things I need to explain to you," he said with no emotion whatsoever. That made it all worse.

"No, you have nothing to explain. I got it. I just want to be left alone." Moose Hills sounded perfect right now. Planning fundraisers at libraries and beating up my best friend in a moose costume was so much better than this. I'd left my moose costume to come here to see my kids. My boys. The thought of them had me on the verge of panic.

"They're fine. I have someone looking out for them," Zane added as if he could read my mind.

"What do you mean, looking out for them? Is that a threat? Are you threatening me with my children?" I balled my hands into tight fists, ready to swing if he so much as made to threaten my boys. Although he was bigger and probably could squash me like a bug.

He sighed and raked his hand through his hair. "When you want to hear my explanation, join me in the kitchen. I'm making breakfast." With that, he left me alone in the room.

I had two options. Be reasonable and listen to his explanation or run. If he wanted me dead, he could've killed me and buried me in Maine. And again, he had the chance to end me when he drugged me. I didn't think he wanted me dead, but my instincts weren't really all that great. It wasn't that I'd trusted the wrong people. My problem, as Rosa had eloquently put it, was that I trusted *everyone.*

I pulled back the thick curtain on the window to look outside and saw nothing but a thick wooded landscape. We were in a cabin in the middle of the woods. Angry, I shoved the curtains closed again and stormed out of the room.

Assaulted with the scent of food—bacon and eggs—my stomach rumbled. Of course. I hadn't eaten since lunch.

"Sit down before you fall," he said without turning to me.

I quickly scanned the small space. Larger than my cabin in Maine, but not by much. His entire being screamed he didn't belong in a place like this. With me. He must've been slumming in moose country, Maine. I didn't move. Slowly, he placed two plates loaded with food on the counter in front of him. The act was so domestic that I had to consider him drugging me to be part of my wild imagination. I'd wanted this very moment back in my cabin, to wake up next to him after the night we'd had sex. I'd woken up alone instead. Loneliness had caught up with me that morning. Considering a life with someone else, let alone a man, this man in particular, had been ridiculous. I'd preferred to be alone. Happier without anyone. *That* lie tasted foul on my tongue.

As if he hadn't just lied, cheated, and kidnapped me, he picked up the plates with the utensils, and carefully set them down on the small square table. Then he pulled out a chair. "Sit," he said again, motioning to the pulled out chair. When I didn't move, he added, "Please."

With no other option presently available, I sat. He returned to the kitchen and brought a pitcher of orange juice and some glasses. Once everything seemed perfect for breakfast at three in the morning, he started to eat. Warring with my stomach to not give in to this food temptation, I resisted eating and just watched as he chewed, swallowed, and licked his lips, all the while his eyes remained on me. "It's not poisoned. And I know you're hungry. I can hear your stomach. Eat."

"Then talk," I said, needing to have some control over this ridiculous situation. Starving myself was juvenile and a dumb move. Especially if I'd be forced to escape. I needed all the energy I could get.

"What would you like to know first?"

"Why is there someone watching my kids?"

"Just as a precaution. I have enemies that would use anything to hurt me."

"Why would hurting my kids hurt you?"

"It wouldn't. But it would hurt you and that would hurt me. Now eat."

I'm sure the food wasn't poisoned and may even had been delicious if I didn't have a stone wedged into my stomach. I tasted nothing but ate anyway.

I used the silence to settle my nerves and form coherent thoughts. Once we were done, he got to his feet and started to clean up the plates without saying a word. Silently, I helped him. It wasn't until everything was clean and put back that he finally turned to me.

"You said you'd explain things. Why am I here?" Standing just inches from him, I had to lift my head to look at him. The guy was tall and powerful. Calculating. As if he were measuring his words before he decided to talk to me.

"My family has certain interests that enemies would like to take away from us."

"Like a crime family? Are you a mobster?" He nodded, though his eyes remained expressionless. None of this made any type of sense. "And why would I be of any interest? Are all your one-night stands at risk?" Thinking about all his one-night stands made me regret eating.

"No," he answered dryly.

I waited for more information that didn't come. "That's it. That's all you're giving me?"

"You might have a target on your head."

"Might? Means you don't really know."

"No. I don't really know."

I almost wished that this was some kind of ploy he concocted to force me to stay with him. The alternative would be that he was telling the truth and me and my kids were in danger. Which made no sense unless there was something more he wasn't telling me.

"So what was your big plan? Keep me here indefinitely?"

Leaning against the counter, he crossed his arms in front of his broad chest. "I hadn't really thought it through. I hadn't had time to think clearly since I saw you with that *human*."

It took me a second to realize he meant the cute bartender. "Is he okay? You didn't hurt him, did you?"

"I did not," he squeezed out between his teeth.

"Thank you for your consideration for my safety, but you can take me home now."

He clenched his jaw, grinding his teeth for sure. "You're willing to risk it."

"You're willing to risk it by bringing me here. I'm safer far away from *you*." My anger sifted through the last part, and Zane was on me in a heartbeat. My ass pressed against the sink as he crowded my space.

"Do not underestimate my need to protect you, Eric," he practically growled out. "Do not underestimate my need to make you *mine*."

I should've been afraid by those words. Instead, heat rippled through my body and my cock got hard. Instinctively, I rutted against him, seeking friction on his thigh like some sort of horny teenager unable to control himself. The friction made me grind my teeth to keep from moaning. The guy was engaged. Going to be married, and here I was throwing myself at him. Wanting him to kiss me, to hold me, and maybe even fuck me. I was no better than Pedro who had shoved himself between Layla and me and had stolen her from me.

Angry at myself, at him, at this whole situation, I shoved him back and quickly recovered, distancing myself from him. "I don't belong to you or anyone. Now take me home."

"Bennett will be back at dawn. Rest. We'll leave then." With that, Zane bolted out of the cabin and slammed the door shut behind him, leaving me suddenly feeling guilty for making him mad. I'd done nothing wrong.

Nothing.

I rushed back to the bedroom and slammed the door just for good measure. Then I dropped onto the bed and hugged the pillow. Guilt gnawed at my insides. I hadn't known he was a lying cheat. My body's reaction to him wasn't my fault. I could ignore it. Hell, I'd been ignoring my needs for the better part of twenty years. In a few more hours, I'd be finding a new place where Sebastian and I could hide from the world. Zane forgotten. A learning experience not to trust anyone.

Hugging the pillow tighter, the scent of dry earth and peppermint filling my senses. His scent. I closed my eyes and dreamed of Zane kissing me right before he buried me alive.

Chapter Seventeen

Zane

If I hadn't walked out of the damn cabin, I would've torn it down plank by plank. Eric Diaz wanted nothing to do with me, and I couldn't blame him. I could no longer read into his emotions because they meant shit. People often hurt the ones they loved, cheated on the ones they swore to respect, and killed for pleasure.

The solitude of the mountain always calmed my soul. Nothing around for miles but narrow roads and thick trees. The balance of nature made this place perfect. Unlike human interaction, animals were truer to their nature. The space and cloak of darkness allowed me to push out some of the chaos writhing inside my soul. Its power rippled through me, disturbing the air around me and allowing me to breathe. Sentinel would help strengthen the barrier against the evil chipping away at my sanity. One miscalculation and I would be ripped apart. My error would mean Xcian would have to carry this burden. If not Xcian, then my son.

So damn tired, I shut my eyes, lifted my face to the night skies, and inhaled. I caught Eric's scent in the air. A scent that soothed me and made me feel everything. Then there was something else. A dangerous presence that would continue to follow me until the end of days.

Finnegan.

"He *is* beautiful," Finnegan's voice reeked of sexual tension. "I can see why you chose him."

I hadn't *chosen* Eric, though. Choosing had been left out of the equation for us when it came to a binding union. It had been left to the Fates. Finnegan knew this on a cellular level because he had bound himself to me while I could not return the emotion. The one-sided tether had made him unstable and batshit crazy.

"It's only temporary," I lied. "I'll use him the way I did with the others and then toss him away."

Finnegan moved like a predator circling its prey. But I was no longer prey. He'd taught me how to control my resolve, how to lie and cheat. He taught me how to manipulate to get what I wanted. And he also taught me how to relieve the chaos inside of me.

When he came upon me, he wore Eric's face. I startled for a second at the near-perfect image in front of me of the man I wanted to bury myself inside. Except, the copy was still Finnegan. An illusion. There was no spark coursing through my veins with a need for him, and his scent was all wrong. Not even wraiths could manage the perfect copy.

"Does this do nothing for you?" he asked.

Even in the dark, I could tell the distortion. Eric's eyes were lighter and every time he stood close to me, his body would pulse with lustful need. I sensed no such thing from the copy.

And the wraith knew it.

He quickly returned to the image he had bound himself to. Dark hair and even darker eyes framed by thick lashes with androgynous features.

Though Finnegan made my life harder than

necessary by binding himself to me, he'd tethered us so that he could not bring me harm. Whether he liked it or not, he had become vested in seeing me survive my union. Unfortunately, wraiths were harder to kill than I thought. After drowning, skinning, and beheading Finnegan, the wraith still managed to return to me.

"Why are you here? I doubt you came all this way to watch me play with my pet."

Finnegan smirked though his eyes remained unmoved. "I'm hearing you like to keep more than one pet, *mi amore*."

I flinched at the term of endearment.

"Instead of playing with this one," he went on, "you should ensure the protection of your betrothed. Has it not ever bothered you that you have yet to secure a union? Your females seem to find an early demise right before your wedding."

I swallowed the lump in my throat. The malice had said the same thing. "What do you know of it?"

Finnegan purred and ran one long, cold finger down my cheek to my throat. Dark eyes full of hatred followed the trail he made. I was taller than him, much larger, and could rip his head off his shoulders just to spite him, but I remained still. An effort that cost me dearly. "Now, now, where would the fun be in telling you?"

"It means you don't know shit," I hissed out.

He dropped his hand and shrugged. A movement that made him look more human than his altered features. "I only need to keep you safe."

"Until I'm bound. Then you'll have to keep *us* safe."

Jealousy speared through Finn, and he cupped my

throat, squeezing. I still didn't move, allowing him this one breach. "Do not tempt me to return you to Hell, Zane," he spat out. "I may not be able to have your soul, but I can still make do with your body."

My blood ran cold at the thought of returning to Hell. Pulling on my anger to make me stronger, I slammed into him, sending him flying back. He hit the ground hard, and I was already on him before he regained his senses, lifting him by the throat. "Do not threaten me, shadow stalker. I am no longer that youngling incapable of defending myself. You should remember that."

"Zane?"

Eric's voice brought me back to reality. Finnegan gave me a knowing smirk. One that said he knew how much Eric meant to me. He'd felt it through whatever tainted connection we had. "Leave, or I will return *you* to Hell." I released him. He gave a slight bow, his hatred unbound, then disappeared.

I fisted my hands at my side as memories of my time in Hell threatened to tear the protective wall around my soul. I couldn't let it in. I just couldn't. My body coiled tight, needing a fight, a relief. Something.

That something just stepped beside me and touched my arm. The skin contact drew sparks underneath my flesh. I almost buckled at the amount of strength it took not to taste his lips, his soul.

"Zane, are you all right?"

"No," I said simply. I'd never be all right. Eric's fingers drew a path down my forearm until he clasped our hands.

"Come inside. You're cold."

The gentleness of his voice calmed my soul. Once

inside, he quickly locked the door and led me to the sofa, where he wrapped a warm blanket around my shoulders. I should've snapped out of my melancholy. I shouldn't have allowed the past to haunt me. But being on the precipice of my union, all I could think about was my time in Hell. Lucifer's burning touch against my skin. His cold, soft lips pressed against my mouth. And the insanity that followed.

I blinked away the haze that threatened to enrapture me in another time and place as Eric kneeled in front of me. He handed me a warm cup of what smelled like hot chocolate. "I found some chocolate in the cupboard. The only thing not expired." He cupped my hand and led me to hold the warm cup with both hands. "Be careful, it's hot."

I sat dumbfounded, staring at the steam rising from the cup. Leander had liked chocolate. The only reason I had purchased some, but Leander hadn't set foot in the cabin since I'd rescued him from the malice that had taken him. Another one of my many errors that cost someone I cared about much pain.

Finn did what he set out to do. He left me broken in the past. Except I wasn't alone this time. I was with this kind, loving man whose kindness tore away at every shield I placed around my soul. The man who I'd hurt.

"I don't love her," I said. "She doesn't love me either."

"Excuse me?"

I lifted my eyes from the steaming cup to the man still close enough to touch, and yet it felt like a crater had formed between us. And I had to narrow that gap somehow or lose myself.

Chapter Eighteen

Eric

After the third time I'd been buried with kisses by Zane in my dreams, I decided to get out of bed. I found hot chocolate in the kitchen and mixed it with water— no milk available. That was when I felt the ground tremble slightly as if a truck were rumbling past. I saw Zane just outside, and he looked frozen in time, staring into the thicket of trees. Shadows swirled around him while a gentle breeze stirred the leaves. But Zane wasn't under the trees, so the shadows made no sense. I blinked a few times to try to clear my vision. A strange pull compelled me to him. He was hurting. Not physically, but internally. It was as if he'd sent out a silent scream for me. I was dreaming. The only thing that made sense. Zane was driving me nuts.

Calling his name hadn't stirred a response, not until I touched him. Yes, I was angry at him for using me to cheat on his fiancée. Yes, I was angry at him for drugging me and bringing me to this place, but it didn't mean that I didn't care about him.

Whatever he saw out there still clung to him as I sat him down. It was clear in the graveness of his blue eyes. The paleness of his skin. And then he said what I had hoped deep inside my black heart to be true.

He didn't love her.

She didn't love him.

Did that make it any better?

I wasn't so sure I wanted an explanation anymore. Would it matter? Relationships couldn't be built on lies. One night of passion was all we've been afforded. Whatever reason he had to bring me here had been altruistic. He hadn't hurt me. He wouldn't hurt me. He'd take me back home and we'd go our separate ways. The thought didn't make me feel better. I started to move away when his hand gripped my wrist. Hard enough to stop me, but not to hurt. He leaned forward, placed the hot cup on the table, then sharply pulled me closer. A surprised sound escaped my throat. The forward movement forced me to straddle his thick thighs. My hands landed on his shoulders while his were on my waist in a hard grip. He smelled so damn good.

"Serena and I have been betrothed since she was ten years old. She's a good friend to me and our families would benefit from the marriage."

I tried to wiggle out of his grasp, but he held me tighter. "Jesus, you make it sound like a business deal. Is that what marriage is to you people?" Getting nowhere, I stopped squirming. "Can't you just say no?" A tinge of jealousy filtered out of my voice. I had no right to ask that question.

Yeah, that was a total lie.

"There are consequences to negating the union. It wouldn't end well for our families or for her."

For her.

Unrestricted jealousy coursed through me. It was easy to believe I was being set aside for someone else. For Serena—*her*—the beautiful woman he'd been content to grind against just a few hours ago while I'd been mourning the loss of him and my dog for almost four months. That he had me questioning everything about my sexuality, never mind. I wasn't afraid to explore things about myself in private. But I'd done more than explore. I'd gone all out and had sex with a man. A man. And loved every minute up until he left like a thief in the night. Hell, I wrote bestsellers with this shit. I should've known better. He discarded me without a second thought. I deserved someone who loved me. Just me. Who wouldn't cheat on me as Layla had done for months!

Panic set in, and I was pulling away when he cupped my face. The warmth of his touch had tears spilling out of my eyes, down my face like a heartbroken, pathetic idiot.

"You do deserve better, Eric," he said as if he read my mind. "You deserve better than me. Better than this. It was why I walked away from you."

"And now you're trying to manipulate me into believing I need you to protect me. Really? Do you think I'm that pathetic?"

Oh, God, he did. His silence said it all.

With a grunt, I broke free and stumbled away from him. He didn't move from his position on the sofa. The chocolate had been forgotten on the coffee table.

"I'm sorry."

"Sorry doesn't change anything. Answer me this. Were you engaged to her when you came to me in Maine?"

"No," he said, and my heart burst into flames.

My follow-up question would've been why me, but it didn't matter anymore. He had chosen to go through with the betrothal *after* our day together. It meant that I wasn't enough. He had chosen her over me. I turned, fled to the bathroom, and made it just in time to spew out breakfast.

What had I been thinking? One day of being with someone did not make a relationship. He knew this woman far longer than me. I knew him for two seconds. With one quick motion, I wiped my face from the tears and laughed. The ridiculousness of it all had me giggling like a fool.

Bennett was waiting outside with the car when I got out of the bathroom. Zane looked as if he'd been buried alive in real life and not just in a dream. I tried not to read too much into that, but my imagination was a bitch with a bazooka.

"I won't be able to protect you if you decide this," Zane said, despondent.

Not what I'd expected him to say. Our parting words. "Good," I snapped back.

He sighed. I ignored him and slipped into the car.

We drove through the narrow blacktop flanked by trees for the hour drive back to Alejandro's place. I hadn't even given him the address. A telltale sign that he had someone close. Maybe a threat. I didn't do well with threats. Unlike Sebastian, who lived in a dorm, Alejandro had shared a house with three other students who also graduated this week. By the look of the dark house, it seemed as if they were either asleep, or gone. Bennett stopped the car just at the curb. "If I learn that someone is following us, I will call the cops," I threatened.

"Get out of town, Eric. Take your kid and go to New York or fucking Alaska. Just get out of LA."

I snorted and shook my head without giving him a look. I didn't want to give him the satisfaction of knowing how much he'd hurt me. Though I was pretty sure he knew that already. "Have a good life, *Thomas*." I reached for the door but didn't make it far when he grabbed me, pulled me into his hard body, and slammed his mouth against mine. The kiss was feral. Something raw and visceral. His tongue delved into my mouth, exploring every fraction, tasting me while I tried to keep up. Heat poured into my veins as my lizard brain took over. Blood rushed to my cock in a painful pulse as he sucked on my lips, my tongue. He nipped hungrily. His chest vibrated as though purring, trying to maintain some semblance of control while I totally lost it.

The scent in the car was a heady mixture of musk and the aftermath of a rainy day under a blanket of trees. Of him. Of us. A delicious fire ravaged my body. It was intoxicating. Drew all my nerve endings to attention. His fingers dug into the back of my hair, pinning me in place. The world around me turned into a single point of just us, of him. Nothing else mattered. The control I thought I had against this man shattered.

Mine.

He had claimed me.

A hint of pain turned to a cool pleasure as a moan escaped my mouth. His warm hands cupped my face as the kiss melded into something sweeter, softer until he pulled away. I chased his lips, needing to taste him again on my tongue. Needing to feel his skin against mine. Needing more. A whimper fell out of my mouth at the immediate loss of him. The sound brought me back down from my temporary insanity. Our bodies pressed together, my leg propped on his thigh, and Bennett like a stone guardian ignoring it all. Oh, God. It had only taken a single kiss to turn everything I believed in upside down. One kiss and I'd been turned to a damn weeping mess, knowing how it all would end.

I dropped my forehead on his shoulder waiting for the dizziness to pass. "This isn't me," I whispered.

His hand gently smoothed the back of my hair. "I know."

"I don't deserve this. I deserve better."

"I know."

I shook my head, embarrassed to face him. "I wish I'd never met you." Without looking at him, I quickly jumped out of the car and slammed the door shut.

Everything I'd learned about taking control of my emotions, about not caring what people thought of me and living my best life had shattered in one weak moment. I needed intervention. Rosa was going to have a meltdown. I lifted my hand to knock on the door and stopped, my fist hanging in the air. The deadbolt had been splintered; the door hung ajar. Slowly, I pushed the door open when a strong hand grabbed my wrist and savagely yanked me inside. Pain blew me apart as my face connected with the hardwood floor. Then a boot landed on my ribs, ripping the breath out of me. Someone savagely pulled the back of my hair until I stood upright.

"You finally made it," the cool voice said into my ear.

"Touch him again and I'll kill you." Zane stood in the doorway, looking dangerous. Even I felt a slight tingle of fear rise up my spine.

I heard a gun cock, and the barrel pressed against the back of my neck. "You want to test your speed?"

Please don't. "Where are my sons?" I croaked out.

"Oh, they're going to meet you in Hell," the terrible voice said.

No. No. No. Please, God. They couldn't be dead. An icy chill encompassed me.

"Go ahead, *demon,*" the man hissed at Zane. "Make your—"

I was suddenly free of the man's hold and my shaking legs dropped me to the cold, hard floor. For the second time in a few hours, the world of darkness greeted me, and I jumped in willingly.

Chapter Nineteen

Zane

The kiss.

The damn kiss had distracted me. It had masked the threat, the scent of the malice. The kiss had done something else. It left no room for argument that Eric belonged to me. Being with him eased the pressure against my soul of the evil threatening to burst. Kissing him had joined us in a way I'd never felt before. A stirring in the most basal portion of my soul had awoken something primal inside of me. I had shared of myself with him, and he hadn't been the wiser.

I wiped my hands with the towel Bennett handed me, leaving it stained with blood. Not mine.

The idiot hadn't known I was faster than a fucking bullet. My phone pinged and I lifted it to my ear already knowing who was calling even without looking at the caller ID.

"The house has been compromised. I have the kid with me."

"You're too fucking late, asshole," I told my brother, grateful that he wasn't in front of me. "There was one waiting here for Eric. You are so fucking lucky he came out of this alive or I would've fucking ripped your fucking dick out of your fucking body. Tell me I'm lying. Just tell me."

Xcian said nothing. Smart man.

"Which one do you have?"

"Sebastian," Xcian said, with a lot less snark in his voice. "The other one took a flight out to New York this morning."

"Good. Send a cleaning crew to wipe his house and take the boy to the mansion. They're involved now. We have to tell Father."

"I don't think that's a good idea, bro. You know what happens to humans when they venture into our world."

They disappear.

I turned to look at Eric, still passed out on the sofa where Bennett had put him because I couldn't even touch the man without sending sparks into the electrical system of the house. "He's my chosen, Xcian."

Another stretch of silence followed as I let Xcian absorb that. "He must agree for Father not to harm his blood."

Fuck. I knew that too. If Eric refused to bind with me, either he'd be killed by another malice or by my father who would see him as a threat to our kind. And I knew Eric would never agree to be with me while I was mated to Serena. Having an heir had always been my fate. At least I'd be able to protect my son. I wouldn't be able to do the same for Xcian. My father would be responsible for my brother the same way he'd been responsible for me. And he'd done a piss-poor job of it. Either way, Eric had no choice now. Either be killed or fall under my protection. Those were his only two choices now.

"Eric will agree when he learns what's at stake. Make sure the kid knows that he'll see his father so long as Eric agrees to my terms."

"He'll hate you for it."

"So be it. Take the kid to one of our safehouses. I'll call you with instructions." Before Xcian could say anything, I ended the call.

Bennett watched me silently. "Are you sure you want to do this? He could remain clueless, and we can still protect him."

"For how long? Until time takes him away from me?" I couldn't even think of him aging and dying. That's exactly what would happen if he didn't agree to bind with me. The lights flickered. "No. He will agree to be mine or he will lose his children before he loses his life. Those are his options."

"As you command, sire," Bennett said in a condescending tone.

"That is what I command. Now, take him and make sure he's secured. There's something I have to do."

I could tell Bennett had more choice words to say, but he'd kept them to himself. Ten minutes later, Hawke answered my call, and we drove to Serena's penthouse. Of course, the moment I stepped out of the private elevator into her loft, she was ready for me.

"You sonofabitch. You couldn't wait until we were married!"

"Well, I'm glad you are well." I flinched, thinking she was going to tackle me to the floor and beat me silly. Instead, she wrapped me in a hug. "You asshole. I told you this wouldn't work," she whispered into my ear right before she punched me in the gut, anyway.

"How did you know?" I followed her to the bar, rubbing my stomach.

She proceeded to battle with the bottle of wine

until Hawke took it from her hands, easily uncorking the bottle as she glared at him. He poured two fingers into her glass and four into mine.

"Xcian called me to convince me to convince you that you are making the biggest mistake of your life."

Too late.

She took a hefty swallow of her drink. "Do you love him?"

I loved him five years ago when I met him, and he doesn't even remember me. I didn't say that because it was not about love. Love wasn't a word that defined what our kind felt when we bonded with another. It was a soul bond, a life oath. It was everything. To ignore it would be to live life in the void, hollowed out and empty. Fuck, I wanted to scream.

"That bad?" She gave me that puppy eye look as she walked around the counter and met me for another hug. "I'm so happy for you. Not everyone finds love."

Hawke made a frustrated sound and walked away. He didn't go far, just far enough not to listen.

"You are such a sap. This is not a good thing. He's going to hate me."

"Then let's call off this charade. We both don't want this."

"I can't do that to you, Serena," I said, taking her petite, yet strong hands in mine. I had always wanted to love her like a man should, completely, body and soul, but beyond friendship, there was nothing.

"You know the binding might only be one way, Zane. The reason Finnegan does not hold half your soul."

I did know that. Eric would hate me for forcing him to take my protection. He'd hate me for keeping him a prisoner by my side while I married someone else. I'd felt his anger and pain when I told him I'd chosen Serena over him. That had been my first mistake. The biggest lie of all. I knew then that he would never fully give his heart to me. Not when I shared a life with someone else. The concept of marriage to humans was something other than biological. It was something sacred. At least for Eric it had been. And he knew firsthand how it felt to be cheated on. To be discarded. He'd gone through too much with his ex to believe whatever I offered him was real.

Serena's soft hands touched my face. "You carry the burden of us all. Are you sure you have to?"

The thought of Xcian with Lucifer in Hell drove needles through my skin. For him to be tethered to a wraith made it all unbearable. "I have to do this for the sake of my brothers," I whispered so Hawke wouldn't hear.

Serena wiped my tears with the pads of her fingers. "Then I'll convince this man that you are the true deal. We don't have to have sex. Artificial insemination is a thing."

I smirked and kissed her palm. "I love you, you do know that, right?"

"Yeah," she said, and I didn't miss her eyes lifting to where I knew Hawke watched us. Because had it been her choice, she would've chosen my brother instead of me.

"But that's not how this works. I should've explained it to you earlier, and for that, I'm sorry."

She blanched and returned behind the bar reaching for another refill. I didn't blame her. "So how will this work?"

"In order for the Anunnaki to keep the demons locked up, we have to create a barrier within our headspace." I rubbed my jaw just to give myself a moment to consider how to phrase everything. "This representation can be a moment, a scene, something that grounds us. Something good to counterbalance the evil inside of us. This place in our mind just happens. I don't know how. Our true mate, our bonded mate, is the only one that can find us there, and if they agree to the binding, if their feelings are pure, they are allowed inside to take their place beside us. We share our power with them to alleviate the pressure inherent in keeping the demons out of this world."

"And if the person refuses, like you with Finn?"

I almost rolled my eyes because everyone knew that fucking story. "If the person refuses, we go mad until we pop like a balloon, releasing the demons back into the world, destroying our vessel. We'll be reborn through our parents with little to no memory of our past lives."

"That sucks. The gods couldn't make it a little easier?"

I snorted. "They wanted to ensure that we had a human connection to this world. Vested in protecting it. So we're born, not made."

"Can you force it, the binding?"

"No. A forced binding is tainted. It'll still drive me mad until I pop."

"And you believe Eric is your true mate."

"Yes," I answered without hesitation. "But I can't have an heir with Eric. The new cycle of warriors will be bred by us, you and me. And our union has to be…intimate." This whole shit felt so damn wrong. "I won't take you by force, Serena. If you choose not to go through with this, I'll have your back."

She gave me a soft smile. "I know, but who will have yours?"

Fuck, she was the female version of Eric. Kind, beautiful, caring for others, but she wasn't him.

"So," she said breaking me from my thoughts. "You don't have to be bound to me. Just get me pregnant."

"Yes, that's correct. We can't conceive with just anyone. Your bloodline is a match."

She sighed, resting her chin on her palm. Too damn young. Too damn innocent. Neither of us ready for this shit. "Does it have to be you? I mean, can one of your other brothers take the reign and be patriarch?" Her eyes instinctively went to Hawke again. My idiot brother.

"Any one of us could step up to be patriarch, but as the eldest, I was chosen."

She swallowed the rest of her wine. "So no artificial insemination option." She gave me a slow smile.

How I wished I could've loved her as much as my idiot brother. "No. I'm afraid tradition rules in this instance."

"Then you're probably going to want to keep that between us. Not sure if your human mate will be so willing to accept your soul if he knows about it." She tapped my hand as if I were screwed. I *was* screwed.

"We have another problem," I said loud enough for Hawke to hear. He pushed away from the wall he'd been holding up and approached us.

Serena lifted her finger to stop me from talking as she poured herself another portion. "Okay. What?"

"Someone is sabotaging my union by killing my soon-to-be brides."

"That malice was bullshitting," Hawke growled out. The energy in the room cackled with etheric energy pulsing from my brother, who had inherited Uncle Simon's flair for giving people nosebleeds right before their heads exploded.

I wiped my nose to be sure and Serena did the same.

"Finn echoed our malice's mention of the deaths of my betrothed. I don't think they died of natural causes or accidents."

Hawke started to pace. "Then we should push up the timetable of the union. Get it over with."

Serena snorted. "No."

Hawke rounded on her. "Why not? You can't stop the inevitable. Getting it over with sooner protects you."

"I'm not even sure I want to get married!"

"Too late. You already agreed."

"Agreed? Is that what you call being threatened to be thrown to the wolves if I didn't do this? An agreement!"

"Yes! The choice has been made and you're getting fucking married!"

This was one argument I did not want to stick my nose in. I'd be at risk of losing it. But Hawke was right. If Serena didn't go along with the union, she'd be exiled by my family who had purchased her. Unprotected, she'd be hunted.

"He's right, Serena," I said.

She glared at me. Understanding dawned on her expression. Instead of arguing, she stormed into her room, slamming the door behind her.

"Stay with her. Make sure you keep her safe."

Hawke nodded.

Chapter Twenty

Eric

"I know it doesn't feel like it now, but sometimes our heartbreak only clears the way for something better. It cleanses us." The heat of the man's breath touched the back of my neck. A reminder of how close we were to each other. Lying in a spooning position on a bed in a hotel room.

Layla had finally left me for another man and I'd been kidnapped and taken to a dark hotel room with a stranger who wanted to hug me. And it didn't feel weird or wrong. I snorted at his words. "Put that on a hallmark card." Another sob wracked through me, my vision blurred, my nose stuffed. I hadn't stopped crying since the restaurant.

He chuckled, and I liked the sound of it. His chest vibrating against my back. Despite being fully clothed, I felt his warmth seep into me, relaxing me. For some inexplicable reason, he'd latched on to me and my heartbreak.

"Have you ever had your heart broken?" I asked.

"Once. I lived and breathed for that person, only to get shanked at the end."

"And did you find enlightenment?"

"No. But I found you."

There was an ease of silence as my eyes burned

and I shut them. I had been crying my eyes out when the man behind me kidnapped me. I'd thought he meant to kill and bury me in an unmarked grave. My family would never find me. The horrible part was that I didn't care at that moment. I didn't care that I'd let a stranger drive me to a hotel. I didn't care that my eyes had been so bloodshot and swollen that I couldn't even see his face clearly. My nose was so clogged I couldn't even smell him. The only reason I knew he was real was the feel of his arms around me, and the feel of his breath against my neck. I felt him inhale me as if taking me to scented memory. "You deserve better than her. You deserve someone who loves you and cherishes only you." The deep voice sounded oddly familiar. "You don't deserve a monster."

The voice changed, deeper, until its resonance drew an image of blond hair, ocean blue eyes, and rigid features. "But you got a monster, anyway."

I jolted awake, biting back a scream as the world swam into focus. Like a newborn calf unable to steady its legs, I fell on all fours beside the bed. The memory of the stranger peeled away into a hazy remnant. Memories couldn't pull from something that wasn't there. I hadn't bothered to look at his face because I hadn't wanted to *see*. Just to feel. To sleep. To cry. I had wanted to coward my way through my pain.

Coward.

I felt the echo of the noose around my neck, the sharp pain, and then my chest tightening, unable to breathe.

Breathe. I was breathing. It'd only been a nightmare. My back hit the wall.

I inhaled a breath, then another, and another, until

the white spots dancing in front of my eyes vanished.

Alive. I was still alive. Breathing. Hurting. Pain and I had become intimate over the years. It held me in a vice grip. The racking breaths turned to sobs.

Alive.

A gun to my temple. My boys. The mention of seeing them in Hell. And then Zane there and then gone.

I pressed the heel of my palms against my eyes, hoping to sort out the haze of visuals leaping for attention in my fuzzy brain. I needed to get to my boys. To know they were safe. As my breathing eased, so did the mental onslaught, but not the pain in my body. I finally opened my eyes to the large room decked out in furniture taken out of the Victorian era. Elegant and sophisticated, it looked straight out of a king's palace. The room drew on hues of pale gold and browns, larger than the size of Mrs. Owen's cabin. Brown drapes hung off floor-to-ceiling windows. The pale beam of light floating in from the window indicated that night had fallen.

Using the ivory-colored credenza, I lifted myself. My left side ached. Not broken, but definitely bruised. And my head felt as if I'd been scalped. The tender knot where I'd slammed into the floor seamed with a fresh set of stitches. Using the wall for balance, I found a door that led to an empty closet. Then another that led to the en-suite bathroom. With shaking hands, I turned on the lights. White floors, white porcelain counters, white, white, white. All the white hurt my eyes.

My stomach clenched with nothing to toss. After splashing water on my face, I made the biggest mistake of looking at myself in the mirror. My face looked like a melon. My left cheek was swollen, my lip busted, stitches on my left temple just at the hairline. My shirt, bloodied, and more bruises underneath. It hurt to breathe, to move, to think.

I patted myself, looking for my phone, and wasn't surprised it was missing.

The temperature dropped as Zane walked into the room behind me. Wearing a black long-sleeved Henley that stretched too tight across his broad shoulders and black cargo pants with black boots accenting his very thick muscles, I wanted to hurl. Just hurl. His blond hair laid on his shoulders, the tips still wet from a recent shower. He looked good. And too damn young. What had I been thinking when I took him to my bed? I hadn't been. It had been one moment of sheer insanity that would not be repeated.

We looked at each other in the mirror.

He stopped at the doorway to the bathroom, crossed his arms, and leaned against the frame as if my world hadn't just collapsed.

I turned around to face him. "Where are my sons?" I asked. Surprisingly, my voice didn't crack, though it hurt like a mother to speak.

"They're alive," he said as if that was supposed to mean something.

The little strength I had almost shattered. "Why wouldn't they be alive? What is going on?"

He slowly licked his lips, leaving a sheer gleam on them. My skin blazing with heat the way it did when he had kissed me. My body responded to his presence with a boner. Sex hadn't even been on my mind. He ran his thumb across his lips in thought. "Their future depends on you."

I almost said, I know. That's a father's job. But he hadn't meant this in generalities. He meant it as a threat.

I took an arrogant step closer, as if I could mentally order him to stop bullshitting me with a glare. With nothing else in my arsenal, my stubborn need to protect my kids was all I had. This man could break my neck, impale me with a well-placed kick, or just shoot me in the head execution style. His whole demeanor screamed danger. How had I missed it back in Maine? Right, because while he held my life in his hands, my children's lives, my body preferred to drop him on that ugly white bed and fuck his brains out. His closeness made me bristle. His scent dominated everything. The magnetic pull he had on me made no sense. "What do you want from me?"

Pushing himself off the wall, he approached me, and I had to back up until my ass hit the sink. I leaned back as he leaned forward, one leg between mine as he pressed his body against me, my traitorous cock hard on his thigh. This was a powerplay. This was what he wanted. To turn me into his submissive. Not happening. Ever.

I jerked forward with my hips, and he lost his balance. I took that as my opportunity to do something, anything. My imagination ran wild with possibilities. Dropping him to the floor, making him immobile, running away. Yeah, didn't happen. He quickly recovered and spun me around so that my back was against his erection. One of his hands wrapped around my waist to keep me steady, the other on my neck to break it should I become a threat. The guy towered over me, at least a full head, and had at least fifty pounds of muscle more than my scrawny ass. No way I could overpower him. Didn't mean I couldn't fight.

"What the hell do you want with me?"

"Your soul," he quickly whispered against the shell of my ear.

All the blood drained from my body as he lifted his eyes to the mirror in front of us. They were glowing blood red. A smirk did not improve his expression. That smirk said time's up. You are so screwed. He licked the side of my neck. His pink tongue against my skin as if he were getting a quick taste before he totally consumed me. "I can sense your desire, Eric."

The sound of my name on those pink full lips drew more desire out of me. And a shit load of fear. "This isn't real," I whispered. More to myself than for him to confirm anything.

He tilted his hips deeper into me and I felt his cock hard as driftwood. "This is real. As real as it gets."

I tried to shake my head, but he hardened his grip on my neck and ran his thumb back and forth along my jaw. "This can be good if you let it."

"For the price of what? My soul? Fuck you." I said the words with little conviction. A tear slipped out of my eye.

"That's not how this works." His eyes were a pale pink and even that started to dim until the blue returned. "I give you a part of my soul. You just have to receive it."

This was crazy town. "No."

"Don't lie to yourself, Eric. You feel our connection. It goes deeper than attraction, deeper than flesh and bones."

I did. I felt it all. And that scared me. "What does

that mean?"

"I am Anunnaki. One of the nine guardians of this world. You have been *chosen*."

I swallowed. There was no joke in his voice, no mirth in his eyes. He truly believed what he was saying. "What does that mean?"

"It means that you are *mine*."

My body responded to those words. An inexplicable need to give him everything sparked through me. I fought against whatever this was. A curse. A hex. My grandmother believed in *brujeria* and curses. This was something like that. It had to be. "It doesn't matter," I said. "If you force me, I will never forgive you."

My words cut deep between both of us. He leaned his head against my temple. A movement that had me leaning into his touch too before he broke us apart and returned to the bedroom. I was not sure if the theme of this room was Dracula in white, though red would totally ruin the paleness of it all. He pulled out his phone from his pocket just as he reached what should be the exit door. I'd already found the closet and the bathroom.

"Bennett," he said, "are you ready to show him?" Zane's expression darkened for a moment then he said, "Now. He's awake." Before anything else could be said, Zane hung up. "Just remember, this is your decision. Whatever you make."

"If believing that lets you sleep at night, by all means, spill more of your bullshit."

Anger washed the coolness off his features. I felt it like a living, breathing thing writhing between us. Edging toward the fringes of reality, I had to stay grounded or risk losing my mind. Bennett tapped on the door and walked inside with a laptop. He didn't look at me at all as he carefully placed the opened laptop on the extra ugly desk. He gave Zane one last look of doubt before turning the thing on. The image that appeared on the small screen shattered whatever little strength I had left to fight.

Sebastian sat in a twin-size bed, propped against the wall. Head down, his dark hair masking his face. The room looked like a basement somewhere.

"Let them talk," Zane said to someone on the phone.

A couple of seconds later, Sebastian lifted his eyes to someone in the room. I had no audio, but whoever it was, motioned to the video feed and Sebastian looked up as though staring directly at me. "Oh, God, don't do this please," I whispered. "Whatever you're going to do, please. I beg you." I was now rambling and totally at Zane's mercy. I knew this, and he knew this.

I recognized the person in the video with Sebastian. Xcian. Zane's brother. He handed Sebastian the phone while Zane handed me his phone.

"Dad?"

My legs crumpled and somehow a chair had been placed behind me, so I didn't fall on the floor. "Sebastian, are you okay?" The tears were a deluge now. I couldn't stop them.

"Yeah, someone came to the house. I didn't know what to do."

I leaned forward and placed my palm on the screen, willing to give him strength. "Are you hurt? Did they hurt you?"

"No. They said they're waiting for word from you

137

so he can take me to you. Where's Alejandro? Is Alex okay? What about Mom? Dad, what's going on?" Sebastian's tears tumbled, and mine fell too. My sweet, sweet boy didn't deserve this. I'd already made his life a living hell, and I was doing it again. All of it, my fault. I hated myself more at that moment than anything in this world.

I heard Zane say something behind me, but I couldn't catch it. The sounds drowned out by my own verbal abuse. The lights in the room flickered, and the screen on the laptop flickered, losing connection. "Don't worry, Sebastian. I'll make this right. I will."

The laptop died, and I hung my head.

"I know you will, Dad," Sebastian said into the phone. "I love you."

"I love you too."

"Zane," a man's voice said into the phone

"If you hurt my son, I will fucking kill you. Do you hear me? I will find a way to end you."

Fingers tore the phone from me, and I shot to my feet to stare at Zane on the phone. "Yeah," Zane said, and added, "Bring him to the ceremony." Another pause and then Zane's expression darkened. "Fuck you. I know what I'm doing. Just get him here." Zane hung up.

"And Alejandro?" I asked.

Zane called another person. "Send me a pic of him now."

I wanted to die. Zane was not bluffing. Whatever plan he had with me was real to the bone. His phone pinged and he showed me the picture of Alejandro in a bar with what appeared to be his friends. I wouldn't know because I didn't know who his friends actually were. "What about my ex, my mom and dad, are you going after them too?"

His hands shook as he ran one through his hair. "I don't think there's a need to stretch out that far."

"Do you have a family you care about?" I hissed out. "Anyone at all that you are willing to give your life for? Because then you know a fraction of what I'm feeling right now thinking that all of them are going to die because of me. Do you have any idea what *you* set into motion? Do you even fucking care!" My cheeks were wet, and Zane's expression had slipped to what I wanted to believe was some sort of compassion. Maybe guilt, maybe fucking regret. The thing of it all was I had no fucking clue what this man believed, what he felt, what was going through his damn head.

Something dark changed in his expression and he seemed to turn to stone. Something I would love to do instead of snot-crying like an infant.

"I vow to keep them safe so long as you do your part."

I wiped my face with my sleeve and winced at the sudden pain in my ribs. His stoic expression slipped for a moment before he fixed it. "What? You have me. So what do you want, my blood, my soul, my life?" I lifted both hands, offering him my wrists. "Because you've already sliced me in half. I have nothing left."

He took both my wrists in his. The touch shocked me out of my fear and replaced it with a sense of security. A sense that I'd found home. I wanted to melt into his touch, to fill myself with him. The moment was fleeting and gone as soon as I remembered my sweet Sebastian locked in some sort of dungeon after everything he'd been through. I pulled sharply away from him, and he stiffened. "In three days, we will perform a ceremony that will bind us for eternity. Then you can have Sebastian back, but I think you should keep Alejandro in the dark. It's better if he doesn't know the truth."

I had so many questions, starting with the name of his medication, but I swallowed it all back. It wouldn't matter. Crazy or not, here I come. I had no choice. He'd taken everything from me, and I had to make things right.

"Okay," I said.

Chapter Twenty-One

Zane

"Because you've already sliced me in half. I have nothing left."

It took every inch of dark power running through my veins to keep from plunging a blade into my heart. Maybe I'd bleed out. But at least the dark energy would take over and I'd become numb to every emotion Eric had exuded in that room. Although I'd made sacrifices to protect my brothers, a father's love was something I failed to understand. Eric's love for his children knew no boundaries. He'd do what he needed to do to keep them safe, and he'd hate me for it.

Blood of my blood.

"You are an idiot. Let me just throw that out there now before you finish this atrocity binding ritual that will have you killed." Finnegan flared his nostrils at the sulfuric stench rising from my mortar. "If you want to hide him with this stench, a little weed will go a long way."

I bristled at him for just mentioning Eric. "Why are you here?"

Finnegan shrugged. "I'm vested in keeping you breathing, or have you forgotten?"

Finn and I had been through this for the better part of a millennium. Throughout the years, that smile turned from pathetic heartbreak to nefarious purpose. Now, it was just gleeful, which seemed wrong on the demon. I stopped feeling guilty about not loving him back when he turned me into Lucifer to punish me. "You downplay it when you believe it to be love. We don't love like humans do. And he is very much human."

Ouch.

After I'd laid out the terms, which included threatening the lives of his sons, whatever feeling he had for me had exploded into ash I could still taste down my throat. "He loves in his own way."

"Not you. He'll never love you. He'll never understand that he has to share you with a female so you can have an heir. Never understand that he will watch his family die of old age while he lives to be your consort."

The mortar and pestle fell from my shaking hands and burst into red flame before it winked out. Finnegan did not look sorry when he mouthed the word *"sorry."*

"What then?" I asked, exasperated. "What the hell can I do? My heart and soul are a fucking mess, and I am about to inadvertently open a portal that can end the world if I don't take whatever is inside of me and share it with someone."

"Share it with Serena. You love her."

"Not the same way."

"Doesn't matter. You'd die for her. You'd protect her interest. Why is that not love?"

"You know why."

"The sex is not good enough with her?"

I hated the demon. "It's not that simple. Why the hell am I telling you this?" I started to clean up the smelly powder and tossed it into the trash.

"There is one way this might work in your favor."

I dropped my palm on the counter and leaned forward, shutting my eyes and hoping the guy would just go away. Instead, he jumped onto the counter and crossed his legs. "The strongest lines are in the aether. You can take her there and force it. The Fates have no power in the spirit world."

Force it with Serena? The thought of ignoring my feelings for Eric made me sick, and Finn knew it. The grin plastered on his face said it all. He hopped down from the counter and tsked. "You don't want to bond with Serena, do you? Living a life without the man you love would be unbearable." Finnegan's voice took a hard turn to it. No longer playful. As I stared into his pained eyes, I realized he was right. I didn't want to end up like Finnegan. In love with someone unable to love me back.

"I won't tempt Fate," I said, my voice thick with emotion. "And if that would work, why didn't you force *me* there?"

"It wasn't an heir I wanted to have with you," he growled out.

I ducked just as a cleaver sailed over my head. It plunked off the refrigerator and ended up on the floor. Luckily, the asshole was gone before I picked it up.

"What died in here?" Mother asked.

My mother. The matriarch of this little fucked up family. Even my father whimpered in her vicinity whenever she showed her true powers. "Bad potion making."

She chuckled, and it sounded elegant in every way. She cupped my cheek, and I had to lean down to receive her kiss. "You don't need to drug him, sweetie. If he refuses to love you, I'll chop off his head and put it on a pike." She gave me a warm smile that did not match her tone.

"Will Sentinel be there?"

"Of course. A union and a binding. We have no clue how this will all go."

It wasn't how I expected my union with Serena would go. Technically, I should've been bound to her as well. Instead, we would be a threesome and they both were not happy with my decision. At least Serena knew the reasoning enough to forgive me. Eric, on the other hand. Mother plucked a grape from the bowl and tossed it into her mouth.

Since we arrived in Hawaii for the Bloodmoon event, which would be a backdrop for the ceremony, Eric had fortified the door to his bedroom with the furniture and had refused to come out or eat. At least I knew he wasn't dead yet, and he had plenty of water in the bathroom.

"Well," she patted my arm. "I have shackles if you need them."

I restrained myself from rolling my eyes though I hoped I wouldn't need the shackles to restrain Eric. He'd been adamant about seeing Sebastian. Xcian hadn't arrived until early this morning and Sebastian had been too tired to see his father. I anticipated their reunion would be well-received on Eric's end and, hopefully, he wouldn't starve to death before the ceremony.

The thought of something happening to him had the world shifting under me. Before I knew it, Mom had cupped my face and wiped my tears with her thumb.

"Calm, little one. It'll be over soon. You're doing the right thing."

"I'm sacrificing his future for—"

"To save his world. I'm sure if you told him the truth he'd understand."

I shook my head. "I can't. It's too much of a burden."

I felt the heat of her palm on my chest, soothing in its limits. "You carry the burden of us all though you don't have to do it alone. Not anymore."

"He doesn't love me back."

"You don't know that. Not for sure. The ritual will tell us everything we need to know about this man and his true intentions."

That's what I was afraid of. I couldn't do anything to stop it. Father walked in and gave me a hard glare. He wasn't as receptive to my sexual preference as my mother. The whole point in loving someone, in his mind, was to leave a legacy behind. I couldn't leave a child behind with Eric. That was biologically impossible. The only thing we could ever leave behind was our history. The stories told of us. At least until whatever family we had left turned to ash.

"Don't worry about your father. This is a joyous moment for you. You will be bound to the man you love and have an heir with your best friend."

I knew she meant well, but my heart screamed that Eric would never forgive me for this. He hadn't asked me about my eyes that night in his bedroom. He hadn't asked me what I meant about eternity. He'd asked nothing. Would always see me as a monster created in Hell. He'd hate the thought of my public marriage with Serena. And he'd always hate me for it.

But living without him would be so much worse. A part of me, a very deep part of me, still held out for hope. Let the Fates decide. It was all I had left.

Chapter Twenty-Two

Eric

Serena's laugh was infectious. She threw her head back, laughing until her eyes teared up and she struggled to breathe. The woman's long, dark hair fell in perfect waves down her back. Her suntanned skin flawless, and her brown eyes were kind. When she first broke into my room, I'd been pissed and ordered her to leave me alone. After explaining who she was and that she knew what it meant to be forced into matrimony, I still threw her out of my room.

She returned a few hours later and left a plate of delicious sandwiches on the bed. I'd fortified my door with the heavy furniture, so it was a little disconcerting to see her sitting on the edge of the bed when I came out of my shower. Thankfully, I had a towel wrapped around my hips. She was stubborn and kind and made the best tuna on rye I couldn't resist.

The night we arrived in Hawaii for whatever planned crazy ceremony, she'd snuck into my room. We started talking about her stories with Zane. He must've been a lot older than her because she talked as if he were already an adult when they were betrothed. Apparently, that was a thing in the mobster world. She'd met him after Nanny had escaped and she was frantically searching for it in her living room while her parents were entertaining the Crawfords with Zane. He hadn't ratted her out. Instead, he had helped her look for Nanny. It wasn't until he had squeaked like a girl that she knew he'd found it. Her tarantula. According to her, Zane had fainted right there in the kitchen. Needless to say, she'd gotten grounded and betrothed that same night.

"So, he's afraid of spiders," I said.

"Terrified. Like *terrified*." I could hear the love she had for the man and jealousy writhed dark inside of me.

It was endearing listening to stories that made him seem more human and not insane. There was no awkwardness talking to her anymore. She'd arrived with news that Sebastian had made it and that I'd be seeing him soon.

"I don't know Zane the way you do. I don't think I ever will."

She squeezed my hand. "He's a good person, Eric. He does this for a good reason."

"Sacrificing my family in the process. That's not a good person."

She removed her hand and clasped them on her lap. "He'll explain everything after the ceremony."

"And what does that look like?"

She shrugged. "I don't know. I've never been married before."

Shit. I realized that while she was trying to soothe me, she, too, suffered. I wrapped an arm around her and drew her closer. She leaned in slowly and we stayed like that until a knock on the door had us shifting apart as though caught doing something bad.

"Are you ready?" Bennett's voice sounded muffled behind the door.

Serena looked at me. "Be strong and trust your heart." She placed her palm on my chest. My heart rattled but more out of fear than anything else. After we moved the furniture from the door, she swung it open, startling the large man. Bennett smirked. A hint of mirth sparked in his eyes as if he approved of Serena breaking protocol to talk to me.

"Ms. Rushmore," he said.

"Bennett," she said back.

Bennett looked at me and then at the towel around my hips. "Wear a robe and sandals. You will be cleansed with the Elder Matriarch."

Great. Couldn't wait for my mother-in-law to dress me like a little boy. I pulled on a white—yes, I hated the color—robe and sandals, and followed Bennett out. He led me up winding stairs to a third level and unlocked the room to a bedroom as large as mine. This one had an explosion of eggplant color. I didn't care about that, though. My focus centered on the young man resting on the bed, curled on his side, his knees lifted the way he slept when he was a child. With a cautious step, I entered the room. "Seba?"

He lifted his head and warm brown eyes met mine. He was on his feet and in my arms before I was able to move. Taller than me, I had to tiptoe to fully bring him into my body.

"Dad," he said, his body shuddering against mine. At that moment I hated Zane. I hated this family. I hated all of them for making my baby suffer.

"I'm fine. Everything's going to be okay."

Sebastian pulled back, and I cupped his neck just to get a good look at him to make sure he was really well. He smiled and led me to the bed. "What is going on?

Xcian won't tell me anything."

The way he said Xcian's name made a distinct impression as if his jailer was a friend. I took his hand in mine. "Don't trust them, Seba. Please tell me you did not befriend any of them." I felt like a hypocrite warning him against friendship when all I wanted was Zane to love me. That thought made me shiver. Did I want him to love me or let me go? I couldn't decide.

"He saved me, Dad," Sebastian started, breaking me back to reality. "There were these men after us and he saved me."

I nodded frantically, imagining what Seba had been through. "Good. I'm glad."

"What do they want from you?"

The moment of truth. My descent into horrible father of the year. Sebastian had every right to hate me for what I'd done. For what I was doing. But it would protect him and Alejandro. Zane wouldn't hurt them if I did what he asked. I just didn't know how to phrase it so they wouldn't try to save me or fight it. I started smoothing out his hand, feeling his long delicate fingers. Sebastian was always the hypersensitive one, like me. He felt everything in spades. The reason finding my lifeless body after I tried to kill myself had been detrimental for him. I knew he carried that image with him wherever he went, even in his nightmares.

"I, uh, found someone and we decided to get married." Okay, that sounded so lame.

"I don't understand."

"I didn't know he was part of a mobster family, Seba. You have to believe me." I managed to meet his eyes. "Because he cares deeply for me. He feels he could protect us better against his rivals if we get married."

Sebastian scowled. "He?"

Shit. Shit. I wanted the world to swallow me. "Uh, yeah. He. Do you hate me?"

Sebastian smiled. One thing he could never hide from me was his feelings. "No. I could never hate you. I'm happy you found someone. You deserve to be happy. It's just…unexpected."

"I know. Trust me. I know."

"Will I be included in the wedding?"

I really didn't know. "Maybe it's safer if you stay here."

"Well, will I at least get to meet him?"

"Yeah, of course. Um, after."

He gave me a knowing look. "This is all weird, Dad. Do you love him?"

Yes. I did. But I sure as hell didn't *want* to love him. "This is just the best arrangement to be safe. His men are watching Alejandro and he promised to keep us safe. That's enough for me." Sebastian cocked his head trying to figure things out. He wasn't an idiot. I all but said I was being forced into this. "Do you trust me?"

"Yes."

"Then trust me in this."

Sebastian nodded. Bennett cleared his throat. I didn't even know he had stayed in the room. "It's time to go."

I got to my feet and Sebastian hugged me again. "I hope you're doing the right thing," he whispered.

I nodded against his neck before Bennett led me out of the room.

"I hate all of you. I just want you to know that."

Bennett sighed. "I'm sorry it had to be this way."

I bet. We walked through a couple of long corridors and then up another set of winding steps, then down before ending up in an enclosed bath area. Okay, maybe bath area was not the right word. Floor-to-ceiling windows arched into the ceiling revealed a beautiful backdrop of sky and mountainous terrain in the distance. A steaming pool of water stood just under a domed roof lined with pillars. This was how the very rich and infamous lived.

Mobsters.

Although that had been my assumption, there was something deeper going on. Mobsters didn't have evil demon eyes. They were involved in some sort of cult. Nothing made sense in my brain.

Someone was already in the steaming bath.

"I'll leave you," Bennett said and walked away.

I would've run behind him if I hadn't thought my kids were in danger. I turned back to the person in the water and gasped. A wide expanse of back muscles lifted out of the water, then a tight pale ass and strong legs.

Zane.

I'd seen him naked before. Or somewhat. I had been busy trying to sate my desire when he'd been naked under me. But I had a perfect view of all of him and saying he was majestic didn't quite cut it. He'd chopped some of his hair, so it fell just at his neck. Water clung to his skin, hanging on for dear life before dropping to the floor at his feet. I was suddenly thirsty.

He bent down to grab a towel, and I saw the crack of his smooth ass before he covered himself. He turned to watch me drooling. Or I felt as if I was drooling. I didn't check.

His eyes were pale blue, and I wondered if, like a mood ring, they changed colors depending on his emotions. I also realized I knew nothing about him. "I don't even know your full name."

"Crawford. My name is Zane Alexander Crawford." He stood as still as stone. Waiting patiently.

"And you have nine brothers."

He nodded and proceeded to name them. After Xcian, Galen, and Hawke, my mind blanked out.

"And your mother is an Elder?"

He arched a brow.

"Bennett mentioned the Elder Matriarch."

"Yes. Aurora Crawford. My father is Alastair."

"And, uh, they're like you. Anunnaki. Guardians?"

His features stiffened. "You still don't believe me."

I raked my hand through my hair. "How do you expect me to believe you after everything?"

He sighed. "You will believe after the ceremony. Are you ready?"

I felt my body react to his words, and I quickly made sure that nothing of me was sticking out. "I, uh, thought your mother would be here."

God, that sounded awful.

He bowed as if in reverence and kept his eyes lowered when he spoke. "She asked that I do the honor of getting you ready. If you prefer her, I can—"

"No," I said, cutting him off. "No, that's fine. Maybe it's best this way."

He nodded again. The act was so strange coming from him. I'd expected the ceremony to consist of him hitting me upside the head with a club and throwing me over his shoulder caveman style. *This,* this adoration was unnerving.

"Would you like to eat first?"

Thoughts of swallowing a part of him I should not be thinking about rushed through my evil thoughts. My heart's speedometer stuck at fast, my lips parting to ease my breathing. His nostrils flared like a tiger catching the scent of his prey. I watched as he slowly moved to the round table where an assortment of fruits and meats were spread out. Along with wine. I needed wine. Lots of it if I was going to get through this. I walked around the bath and to the table. "I could use some wine."

I thought he was going to say no but he poured me a glass and narrowed the gap between us. I wanted to lick the water from the peaks and valleys of his muscled chest. To taste the saltiness of his sweat mixed with the water clinging to his skin.

I took the offered wine instead. Our fingers brushed, and a jolt of energy shot up my arm. The glass tumbled, shattering onto the floor. As I moved to clean it up, a shard dug into the bottom of my foot, and I winced. Blood quickly pooled and mingled with the wine on the white-tiled floor. My blood. Before I could hop away, Zane lifted me into his arms as if I weighed nothing. I heard the crunch of glass under his bare foot and yet he registered no pain. Nothing.

"Zane, be careful. The glass."

He carefully set me on a chair. "I'm fine," he grumbled and held my bleeding foot. "I'm so sorry. I'm making a mess of everything." He gently plucked out the glass and pressed a napkin to the wound. "I never wanted to hurt you. This wasn't what I wanted. I promise." The vulnerability in his voice shocked me to my core. It contradicted the way he'd been possessive and controlling earlier. All of it so damn confusing.

A shocked silence followed. He wouldn't look at me as he cleaned my foot until I cupped his face and forced his eyes to meet mine. Those startling eyes shimmering with tears set my heart on edge. Zane wasn't my enemy. Whatever he did, whatever he was doing, had to be out of an obligation to something bigger than me. Something larger than us. I couldn't hate him for that. I didn't hate him.

He cupped my hand and turned his head to kiss my palms. Then he propped himself up on his knees between my legs as he ran his hands between my robe, revealing my not-so-muscled chest. Soft fingers explored my bruised ribs, my pecs, my nipples. His mouth followed with kisses. "I'm sorry," he said with every kiss on my body. "I'm sorry."

He suckled my nipples, then lifted higher to kiss my clavicle, my neck, just under my ear. His lips nuzzled along my jawline, and a cool draft made me realize how truly exposed I'd allowed him to get me. My cock jerked as he palmed the length of it. My body was on fire as he continued to rub the pre-cum at my tip with his thumb. Then he lifted his finger to his lips and tasted me.

"Please, Zane. Don't do this to me."

His expression turned completely inscrutable. Guarded. From me. "I apologize. You should bathe. We don't have much time."

A mixture of relief and disappointment struck when he didn't pursue the intimate moment. My foot had stopped bleeding, no pain when I walked around the shards of glass this time and headed to the second larger pool to the left where Zane had appeared from.

"Uh, are you going to disrobe?" he asked.

Right. Because I couldn't bathe in the robe. Then I remembered… "I already showered just before Bennett got me. I don't think this is necessary."

Zane licked his lips, a bit amused. I liked this side of him better than the scary killer or the angry red-eye demon. God, I was insane. "The water is infused with oils and essence. Trust me, you'll feel much better."

I doubted that but I dropped my robe anyway, ignoring the hungry look he gave me from head to toe. Submerging myself slowly into the hot pool drove away all rational thought. The bruising on my body dulled as the power sprays underneath massaged my aching muscles. My worries and stress slipped away. The feeling so amazing. At least until a hard body stood flush against my back. There was no want left to push him away. Instead, I leaned back into his chest as he encircled one strong arm around my waist. His cock digging into my back. The guy so damn taller than me. A moan escaped me as he lowered himself so that his cock slipped between the crease of my ass, sliding against my hole but not penetrating me. All thought of this being wrong floated away.

"What's happening to me?" I asked. "I feel… I feel…really good."

"Just enjoy it, baby," he said into my ear. "Let me wash you."

I nodded but yearned for him to do so much more. I had turned into a vessel of nothing but nerve endings and pleasure. Zane's touch sent a rush of euphoric energy pumping through my veins. The feeling unreal. All of it, unreal.

"This isn't real," I whispered as his hands massaged my shoulders at my back, lathering them with something that smelled like lavender.

"It's real," he said. "Very real."

I couldn't help but giggle like an idiot. "I think I'm high. How could I be high?"

I couldn't see Zane, but clearly heard the smile in his voice. "It's all me, baby."

I snorted. "You think very highly of yourself."

He forced me to turn around to look at him. I felt bubbly and soapy. No, that was just his hands on my chest washing me. Then his hands headed south until he cupped me under the water. I held on to his broad, strong shoulders and hissed out a moan, searching out more friction.

"I think highly of myself?" he said. The subservient guy was gone. Zane was no longer sorry for what he was doing to me and, to be honest, neither was I. "Tell me how I make you feel, Eric," he said, stroking me soft, then hard.

I cupped his hand holding me and squeezed.

"Harder, please," I practically begged. The combination of him and whatever the fuck he'd drugged me with had turned me into a blubbering idiot.

"That's not what I asked," he said, teasing me. His other hand cupped one ass cheek, spreading me and pulling me tighter against him. His lips caressed my neck. "Tell me how I make you feel, Eric," he demanded.

"So fucking good. You make me feel, ah, fucking good." My body jerked. "I'm so close."

That seemed to do it for him. For both of us. Zane popped me out of the water and dropped me onto the

had silver, long hair and pale eyes, his hair was dark and his eyes blue, well, a mood ring of emotions. She had a soft smile and gentle eyes. Though I could imagine she could be fierce if the occasion called for it.

"Come. We need to get you dressed." She took my arm, and we walked through another adjacent corridor. "This is the part where I explain to you what happens, but I think the time is best served by me telling you a little bit about Zane. Is it safe to assume the goofball told you nothing about himself?"

"I heard stories from Serena," I said.

The woman smiled. "Ah, yes. Serena is a lovely choice for him. They have paired quite nicely." My throat tightened with the jealous lump surging its way upward. "Too bad he could never love her."

"Why is that?" I asked before I lost my nerve.

"Because he loves you. Has loved you since he saw you five years ago. He came home with this wretched sunshine following him as if he finally found the answer he'd been searching a millennium for."

She lost me. "Five years ago?"

"Yes," she said. We reached a large room with a dozen people waiting for me. "It's the little moments we learn to cherish, Mr. Diaz. They can grow into something more." She didn't enter the room, and I didn't want her to leave me.

"I don't understand any of this. I feel lost."

She cupped my face, and I felt a charge of hope there. As a mother, she would want what's best for her sons. "It is when we are lost that we can be found."

With that, she released my face and walked away.

Chapter Twenty-Three

Zane

Another room shredded.

Bennett watched with his arms folded in front of his chest as I kicked the broken drawer. After I'd pounded the walls with my fists, tore at the furniture, and shredded the bed, I stumbled into the bathroom to wash away the blood from my hands. Adrenaline swirled down the drain with it. Leaning my forehead against the cool tile settled my mind and allowed my body to heal. The taste of Eric still on my tongue, the way his body became pliant in my arms. The way he'd almost submitted to me. But he fought to take control and started pleasuring himself. My demons practically jumped for joy. *Mine. Mine. Mine.* The thought of him slamming me over the table and impaling me made my cock painfully hard. It was all I could do not to burst at the seams. Eric taking control was the best fucking thing in the world.

But then I fucked everything up. Couldn't even get him into the tub without hurting him. Couldn't process the surge of emotions running through my body. His fear of me. His want of me. Lust, kindness, doubt…all of it so damn confusing. My poor attempt at regaining some control left him hurting. Made me the controlling, possessive asshole that had kept me from allowing anyone into my heart. How was I supposed to be tethered to him when he didn't even know how he felt? How was giving him a part of my soul better than just carrying the burden myself?

I couldn't do this to him. How could I give him centuries of darkness and not mention the demon piece of shit who had tethered himself to me? Although Finnegan had unofficially bonded with me, giving me his own darkened soul in the process, I'd never accepted it, so it just lingered in my peripherals. Once I gave my soul to Eric, Finnegan would be bound to both of us. A punishment of sorts for loving someone who didn't love you back. I felt sorry for the fucker, knowing what it felt like to love someone who didn't reciprocate the feeling. A reminder of the precarious nature of the whole damn thing. It was times like this that I would've preferred to be weak like a human.

The binding could overwhelm Eric with an onslaught of emotions he wouldn't be able to sort through. What if he went insane? What if he died? I slammed my fist against the tile wall, letting the pain of flesh ease my internal suffering. I deserved more suffering than that.

Once finished, I dressed in the customary white sheer robe the ritual demanded. It fell off my shoulders and dropped to my knees but hid nothing of my body. The Sentinel wanted to see how my body reacted to my chosen and my bride.

Fuck. Serena didn't deserve this either.

Maybe I'd die during the cleansing ceremony. That was always a possibility.

"Are you ready?" Bennett asked.

No. I wasn't, but I nodded anyway just before

throwing on the hood to cover my face and following him outside. The soft touch of the warm night breeze against my heated skin offered some comfort. The binding should've been a special occasion, tethering two souls. This binding was a fucking mess.

Eric would claim half my soul, while I'd keep my Anunnaki powers for my son. A child neither Serena nor I wanted to curse with my bloodline.

We stopped under the Bloodmoon. The reason we'd chosen this spot was that it was closest to the moon. As entities of night, the power of the moon shielded us from threats looking to consume us.

I would be at my most vulnerable during the ceremony with only my brothers for protection. The reason they all had to be in attendance. The nine would protect the one.

I stopped near the pedestal holding the oil that would drench my body for the purification part of the ritual. I'd be consumed in flames. A stirring in the field caught my attention, and I looked up to see Serena. She wore white lace, and her thick black hair contrasted with the soft delicate material. Serena was anything but delicate. Her eyes were haunted. I knew she didn't love me. She loved Hawke. If that asshole was any type of man, he'd fight for her. But Hawke never went against our father. Family was sacred to him. Her parents and guards followed her.

To my right, Eric appeared. He wore a black tunic, black slacks, and boots. I felt my body awaken, my cock stirring at the sight of him. There was no question where my needs were placed. My mother had once told me that I was born with two fierce spirits, each in opposition. One female, one male. I could've gone either way.

Eric and Serena looked at each other across the stone pedestal. Strength flowed between them. The Sentinel would prevent the demons from escaping during my vulnerability. The binding and union would go through him.

My parents stepped behind me and released me of my robe, so I stood naked. Eric's chest rose and fell with each deep inhalation of breath, as if he wanted to run. Or stop this. He wanted to do something. I just didn't know what. He didn't have parents or a slew of guards at his back. He stood alone.

Xcian was the first to come forward. He gave Serena a sliver of pine. He said the words of our people in reverence and bowed his head. Then he approached Eric. The man stiffened, and I was almost sure Eric would refuse the same gift, but he didn't. Galen was next as third born, then Hawk, Noah, the twins—Sage and Basil—Zack, Leander, and finally Aristotle, the youngest. The Anunnaki. Defenders of this realm. They stood in front of me in a semicircle.

"With fire, comes truth. In truth, purpose is revealed. In purpose we ascend," my mother said. The words were echoed by everyone but Eric, who now looked as if he were going to pass out.

My parents led me to a small clearing already outlined with a pyre on the ground. I stepped over it and inside. My mom handed me the flagon of oil and then gently kissed me. "Have faith. Your spirit is not wrong."

I nodded at her words and prayed she was right, or I'd dragged Eric into this for nothing. There was still a possibility my spirit would choose Serena. I could've just felt nothing but bodily lust for Eric, nothing more. The control, possessive freak in me wanted him, while my spirit wanted Serena. That was still a possibility. I almost hoped that it would happen that way and I shot her a glance she returned with stoicism.

With a nod, my mother stepped back. My father acknowledged me briefly and stepped away as well. This was the moment of truth. I'd cleanse my spirit and be vulnerable to the etheric energies around me. Lucifer could drag me back to Hell as the flames consumed me. Or everything could go as planned and I could awaken with a sense of calm, joined with my other half. *Please, let it be Serena.*

Xcian gave me a pathetic look.

Here goes nothing.

I lifted the flagon over my head and tipped it. The thick liquid clung to me like sap, cool to the touch. Someone inhaled sharply as the pine in Serena's and Eric's hands ignited. The expression on Eric's face was horrifying. He finally realized what was about to happen. My mother had agreed to explain the ritual to Eric. Born of fire, it would cleanse me, not kill me. But by the look on Eric's face, my dear mother must've skipped that part. The small smile on her face confirmed it.

And that's when the shit turned sideways.

Serena approached me and dropped the flame. With a resounding whoosh, the kindling at my feet ignited, catching the oil along my skin on fire. The immediate sensation rushing through me made me cry out. Not from pain, but from release. The fire lifted all the emotions rooted inside of me away from my soul and, for one moment, I felt free of the demons inside of me. There was no pressure of darkness against my flesh, the regret in Eric, or the heartache in Serena. I didn't feel my father's disappointment in me or my mother's delight. I didn't feel Leander's fear of the night, or Xcian's blame. I felt only *me*. With no link to the ethereal. For one blissful moment, I was just Zane Crawford. It didn't last. Someone cried out. Chaos erupted around me and through the flames I saw Eric rushing toward me, ignoring the screams demanding him to stop. My mother shifted slightly away from him, giving him space to jump into the flames. He slammed into me like a battering ram.

The world exploded as my tether to the ethereal snapped. Time slowed. Darkness cradled me. My power drained. Fighting against the wave of demon energy, I shoved Eric off me hard, and the flames followed him to the ground.

Chapter Twenty-Four

Eric

As soon as Zane screamed, I jumped into the fire.

No one ever charged me with being smart enough to know when not to stick my head out for someone. Stuck in the snow? Yup, I'm the idiot that spends the next half hour in the cold helping you get out. Need a few bucks to make that grocery bill? Sure. Here you go. Even Rosa, my life coach, suspected me of being one big pathetic sap when it came to people in need. So jumping into the fire after hearing Zane scream had only been about satisfying my need to help. I would've done it for anyone. *Anyone*. Not just Zane. Not just because my heart had felt as if it'd been ripped out of my chest and tossed into the fire alongside him. Not because I thought his family was fucking crazy for allowing this to happen. Even Serena had suddenly dropped from the pedestal I'd put her on.

They were all crazy as a moose with a hard-on for baked goods.

Jumping into the fire to save Zane had been all instinct. All drive to save the man who made me consider the relevancy of my sanity. I didn't want to be sane and alone. I didn't want to be sane and live without the thought of Zane in this world. His unbridled laughter back at the cabin, his touches, the scorching looks he gave me. I wanted all of that.

Stop, drop, and roll. All I had to do was stop, drop, and roll.

I did the stopping part well. I'd slammed into an immovable object.

Passing through the flame felt like passing through a beaded curtain. My mother had one of those hanging in the doorway leading to the bedroom because we couldn't afford a real door. Once inside the space, I took a slow, long look at Zane and almost stroked out. The deep lines that made him look scary had smoothed from his features. The scowl he wore so well was replaced by a soft smile that speared my heart. Under the glowing light of the moon, he looked resplendent. That same light enveloped me in his space, tethering us. I felt it like a delicate thread inside my soul, tugging out of my chest and reaching for him. It felt right.

Then doubt sifted through my thoughts like sand in an hourglass. Pouring one after the other. I wasn't good enough for this man. He deserved better than a coward like me. He deserved the moon and stars. His happiness was all that mattered. Emotions became a jumbled mess in my heart. I would've given anything to go back to Owen's cabin and show him my moose. Well, not my moose, but a moose. To walk with him on that mountain range. To see him laugh again.

I ran my hand down his face, grazing his jaw, feeling an electric fire under my fingertips as one thought crashed through every barrier I'd erected around my heart.

I loved this man.

And then Zane shoved me away. I fell hard, and the ground swallowed me.

Consumed by a dark void. The air stagnant, and cool. The pounding beat of my heart pulsed in my ears. No longer in the woods, no longer around people, no longer in my world, I'd fallen into someplace else.

Dead.

Was I dead?

The thought of never seeing my sons again burned through me. I'd done nothing but mourn my losses throughout my life. The death of Layla's love for me. The loss of Sebastian's innocence when he found me with a noose around my neck. Unable to meet Alejandro's standard for forgiveness. And now Zane. The love tainted by what got us here in the first place. His lies. The ruthless way he threatened my boys. If we were to move forward with a real relationship, I'd have to teach him how to be a proper father. No kidnapping. And if I was dead, I'd find a way to haunt him.

Up on my feet, I stood in a stretch of void where darkness itself pulsed. You can't have shadows without light, and I searched for the light source, ignoring the writhing, moving shadows peeling out of the walls. One particular shadow solidified into a human shape. Black spiked hair matching his black eyes watched me from its position. Androgynous features made it hard to distinguish it from male or female. As it came closer, I pegged it for a male since it didn't have the curves of a female, though I could be wrong. Taller than me, but shorter than Zane. This person was long and thin, but not frail.

He walked around, inspecting me. The hairs along my skin stood on end and I had the compulsion to scratch my skin until I bled. My hands curled into tight fists.

"You should not be here." The thing's voice was like listening to insanity. Then he smiled. A look of madness touched his eyes. "You have no clue what you've done, what you've unleashed unto this world." He stopped in front of me. "I warned him of this, but Zane never listens."

The mention of Zane broke me out of my trance. "Who are you?" My voice sounded muffled, as if we stood in some sort of hermetically sealed room.

"I am the Prince's keeper of secrets. Wraith and torturer in His name. You can call me Finn."

"Prince? What Prince?"

"Hellfire. He goes by Luc."

I had died and gone to crazy town. "Luc as in Lucifer? The devil? Am I in Hell? Are we in Hell? Am I dead?" Okay, I had to slow down the speed talking. Something I did when I was nervous and in Hell, apparently.

"This is the gateway. The medium between realms. The aether. And no, you are not dead. Yet."

"Why am I here?"

"You are his *chosen* and Lucifer wants him back. I'm sure he's told you all about his demons."

Demons.

At the mention of the demons, Finn swiped his hand and the walls started to pulse like living human flesh. Cracks along the surface oozed blood. The stench of iron and heat assaulted my senses. The onslaught forced me to gag.

"This is how Zane keeps them out of your world. This is what he suffers, why he needs an heir, and you just fucked it all up for him."

This room, this place, the blood was Zane.

170

Somehow, I was inside him. Seeing what he felt. "I don't understand."

"Of course you don't. You're *human*," Finnegan said disgustingly. "We don't have much time. Make a choice, *human*. Accept the binding and move to the center of his soul to share in his pain or run. Your choice."

The shadows moved out of the way to reveal a domed archway. I felt the slight pull to move in that direction.

The choice was easy.

I moved toward the pull, toward Zane. The darkness spread out against the walls, moving away from me, not touching me, allowing me to see my surroundings.

Demons. At least a dozen caged demons were chained along the walls. Some in cages, some simply chained to the concrete behind them. A couple of cages had been ripped apart as if the demons inside them had escaped. The ones left behind rattled their cages, pulled at their chains, making inhuman sounds that made my eyes water. This was the pain I'd felt inside Zane. His teetering from good to evil in the span of moments. The consequences of protecting *my* world. My boys. Layla. Everyone I'd ever cared about. Should these demons be set free, my world would suffer.

And in the middle of the room, I saw Zane and he wasn't alone.

"I know it doesn't feel like it now, but sometimes our heartbreak only clears the way for something better. It cleanses us." Zane's voice carried in the room despite the squealing demons. He had whispered those words into my ear the night Layla left me. The memories swirled in my head as if they had happened just minutes ago and not years.

Zane had his arms wrapped around me in a spooning position in a hotel bed I recognized. "Put that on a hallmark card," I said. My eyes were swollen, my sobs racking through me. I'd been in so much pain and Zane had been the one to make me feel as if I could survive the break-up. He had made me feel safe. "Have you ever had your heart broken?" I asked him.

"Once," he said. "I lived and breathed for that person, only to get shanked at the end."

"And did it clear the way for something better?"

"I found you."

"Why is that a good thing?"

"You deserve better than her. You deserve someone who loves you and cherishes only you."

I had believed him that night. But then the next morning, he was gone. The days and weeks that followed were torture up to the night I almost killed myself. Given a second opportunity to live, I hung on to life with both hands promising never, ever to give up. But something had always been missing. A part of me, gone.

It'd always been *him.*

On the bed, my memory version started to glow, and Zane absorbed the light, but it wasn't enough. I felt his body draining, the light flickering. Zane dying. A loud clank made me turn to the demon nearest me, the cage buckling, losing its integrity. Soon it would be free.

Share in his pain or run.

Zane needed me to carry some of his burden. To save him. I knew that now. My legs moved through the thick shield of evil. A tangible thing pressing against my skin. The closer I got to Zane, the more the shield lifted. A steady vibration started at the base of my neck, branching out through every cell in my body. I climbed onto the bed, taking my dream version's place. Instantly, he wrapped me in his warmth as if we'd returned to that night. A heated charge grazed every part of our bodies that connected, even through our clothes. I felt his pain, but also his strength as he absorbed what I gave him.

And then Zane set me ablaze. A scream ripped out of my throat. My body burning, oozing on the bed. Muscle and bone turned to ash and there was nothing left but my screams.

On a sharp inhalation of breath, I opened my eyes to a dark room. It took me a moment to come into myself as I listened to my ragged breathing, the cool air brushing against my skin. My unblemished skin. Cinderblock made up the four walls around me, and I smelled the cloying stench of rot.

The lumpy mattress creaked as I sat up. Disoriented, I stumbled to the only door in the room just to be jerked back. I took in my surroundings hoping I wasn't in some sort of dungeon chained by my ankle to a metal ring on the floor. No. This was part of the nightmare with Finn. Not real. My inability to reach that damn door made it real.

I shook my head trying to ward away my thoughts of panic. Of…of Zane.

Was he even alive?

Fire. I'd been consumed in fire. I gave myself a once over, patting my ragged clothes, and found no pain. Even the bruises from the beat down I got back home had disappeared. Gone. I touched my bruised lip and that too had healed.

What the flying fuck?

On the verge of panic, I heard my name and squealed. Far from caring how dorky I sounded. Serena sat on a folding chair just to the right of the cot, propped against the wall. There wasn't even a window in the room. Only part of her silhouette was visible against the dim nightlight someone had plugged into the wall socket. My panic didn't go away.

"What's going on?" I asked. "Zane. Is Zane alive? Is he okay?" My thoughts of him burning, screaming, dying, a jumbled mess in my mind.

"He's fine," she said, and lifted her chin to someone behind me.

Zane stood alive and well. "Where am I? Why am I chained? Where's my son?" All of those valid questions. Except for the one I wanted to ask—*do you love me too? Am I a demon? Can you feel my pain?*

My body tingled in his presence, a need to submit to him completely. I fought it with everything I had. By the angry look on his face, he wasn't too happy with me at the moment. I still had to save my children. Stupid feelings were irrelevant.

"I did what you said." The chain rattled as I moved. "Why am I chained? What happened?" I was in a full-blown panic attack and had to breathe or risk passing out. Zane didn't move. His expression was unreadable, cold. Everything he'd told me about being Anunnaki had been the truth. He wasn't human. None of them were human. Was I human anymore? I swallowed the fear lodging in my throat. "I did as you asked. Now let me see my son." I put as much power behind my words to make it a command. Didn't work.

Zane snorted at my lame order. A hint of anger with a dash of mirth filled his expression. "You do *not* give me orders. And you did not do as you were told. You risked the lives of everyone breaching the circle of flame."

"I...I couldn't let you burn!" That got a slight reaction out of him, but he was too good at acting like a damn robot, so I stopped trying to figure out any deeper meaning to his expressions. "I should've let you burn!" The anger that seeped through my voice made the small room vibrate with energy. Or it was just me shaking like a leaf. I couldn't tell anymore.

"I wasn't burning!"

"Obviously or you'd be dead right now. But how was I supposed to know that?"

The space between his brows crinkled. "You didn't know and yet you jumped into the flames to save me?"

Okay, so he made me sound like an idiot. A suicidal idiot, and I was neither. "I couldn't just stand there and do nothing. You screamed. You were burning. In my world, that's not a good thing!"

"I wasn't burning," he said dryly.

"Yeah, we established that already."

"Didn't my mother explain the ritual to you?"

"You mean you naked, dipped in oil, and fried like a chicken? No, she didn't mention that part to me." I wasn't going to tell him what we actually spoke about. "So, now that we cleared that up, you swore you'd protect us. That I could be with my son."

Zane clenched his fists at his sides. "That can't happen right now."

My blood ran feral. "Why not?"

"He's at a safehouse, Eric. You can trust us," Serena said because Zane looked about ready to burst into flames again. "We're back in California. He's safe."

I spun to her. "Safe from who? *You?* I don't even know what you people are."

That made her flinch, and I felt bad at my words, but my boys had to come first. And I was in a precarious position—imprisoned. I shifted my leg, so the chain rattled. "Trust? Then release me."

She sighed.

"I thought so." Then I turned to Zane. "Now that we also established that your word means shit—"

That's as far as I got when he lunged at me and grabbed me by my shirt before he slammed me against the wall. Pain burst through me.

"Zane!" Serena yelled, rushing toward us.

Zane quickly released me before taking a step back. Too late. I'd already seen the anger and glowing red eyes.

I thought about all the demons he'd trapped in a construct of his making inside his mind. The bleeding, tearing of his flesh. The shared ache and pain between us now. "Are you a demon?" Saying the word *demon* made me feel as if I were fighting against my reality with the one that had been revealed to me. Another world. A layer within a layer that made no sense to me.

"I'm a monster you shouldn't fuck with," he growled out.

Serena put a comforting hand on my chest that didn't feel comforting at all. It felt constricting, but I didn't push her away. I blinked back the tears gathering in my eyes and swallowed the lump in my throat. My boys had to come first. They were all that mattered to me.

"After last night," Serena began, looking from Zane back to me, "everyone thinks you're a usurper. That you used Zane's affection for you to complete the foreshadow binding. It means that you absorbed some of Zane's..." She seemed to look for permission to say what needed to be said from Zane, but he didn't move from under the shadows so I couldn't see his face. "...soul," she finally said. "It tethered you to his life." There was more. I could see it in her expression, but this was all she was giving me right now. At least it was something. I didn't quite understand it completely. But the other option was that I was totally insane. That last night was some sort of techno light trick. The flames hadn't been real. I'd been drugged.

"He doesn't believe you," Zane said.

I really didn't like him right now.

I opened my mouth to tell him, but Serena continued with the explanation. "Doesn't matter. Part of Zane's flame was supposed to have been passed to his heir, his child, and now—"

"I messed it all up."

She nodded.

"Yes," Zane hissed out. I suddenly imagined him with a mouth full of sharp teeth, waiting to rip my throat out. "You fucked it all up and I want to know why."

"I told you why. It was a stupid mistake on my part. I...I..." *I cared too much. I love you and couldn't watch you burn.* Whatever reasoning I had sounded so stupid now. "I made a mistake. We can fix this. Just do the flame thingy again. I'll give it back. All of it."

"You can't, sweetie," Serena said. "The spirit wraith has chosen you to carry it. Zane now belongs to you."

I clearly must've heard wrong. "You mean, *I* belong to him."

"Yes," Zane said, this time stepping closer so I could see the dangerous expression he wore. "You are *mine*."

Those words should've driven terror through me. Instead, it sent blood to my cock that quickly hardened, and I had to bite down hard to keep from moaning. I felt dirty and in need of a scalding hot shower. Strike that, a cold shower. "And Serena?"

She gave me a warm, sad smile. "Zane can no longer pass his inheritance to a child, so I'm free."

That didn't sound like something to celebrate. Especially with the murderous glare Zane shot my way.

Chapter Twenty-Five

Zane

The strike had come out of nowhere with the force of a thousand years of pent-up anger. Pain and stars did not go well together, but I experienced both as I fell on all fours, tasting blood in my mouth. My mother gasped, and my brothers stood around the room like toy soldiers. This wasn't the first time my father had struck me. I'd been seventeen when he beat me within an inch of my life and sent me to Hell, literally, as some last resort, to straighten me up. Cognitive-behavioral therapy borne from hell. Lucifer had quite a lot to teach a seventeen-year-old not yet ascended. He'd taught me how to bleed a soul, how to take their energy and harvest what I needed to survive. Not only human energy, but the energies in other demons as well. The reason I'd been the perfect candidate to imprison the worst of the demons inside of me, keeping this realm safe. To relieve some of the energy bursting at my seams, I needed to bind myself with an heir. Eric had taken that option away from me. Some demons had escaped when he broke through the flame and forced our binding. It'd never been done before. Not by a human. We were in uncharted territory right now.

I'd been my father's prize possession and now his worst nightmare.

Because of Eric.

"You chose *him!*"

It hadn't been a choice in the traditional sense. I hadn't picked Eric out in a line-up and said, Yeah, that's the fucker I want to give half my soul to. That's the one I want to tether my life to for the rest of my unnatural life. That's not how it worked, but during times like this, everyone forgot about the reality of our existence. No one had a choice. It was all sensory output and visceral connections, like some sort of computer motherboard with all the intricate mazes of code and electrical impulses that made no fucking sense. Shit connected on an elemental level that had nothing to do with *choice*. I did not choose to be this way. My mother hadn't chosen to marry my father. That shit had been decided for them the moment they were born. By blood.

He rounded me and gave me one swift kick to the ribs. I bit back my cry. It wasn't my older brothers who came to my defense. I heard Leander's voice speak up closer than he should've been while my father raged. Leander was still human. At seventeen, he hadn't ascended yet. It made him at risk of dying.

"That's enough," Leander said, his voice husky from not speaking much. But when he spoke, everyone listened. "This accomplishes nothing."

I got to my feet between my father and Leander because the only thing I had chosen was to protect my brothers, and I'd die doing it. My father caught a clue and kept pacing. Leander didn't look at me as he returned to stand next to Zack, who gave Leander a reprimanding look that said, *Don't risk yourself, asshole.*

"He is my *chosen*. What's done, is," I claimed, sounding more certain than I felt.

My father stuck his finger up at my face. "Then you better train him well. If I sense he is even breathing next to a malice, I will rip his head off his shoulders."

The threat to my chosen had my body writhing and the darkness surging to the surface. I felt my bones shift, my muscles grow, and my jaw begin to ache as my fangs lengthened. The same darkness I felt every time Eric fought me, every time his life was threatened. The need to protect my chosen at all costs. "You do and I'll die with him."

"So be it," my father hissed.

"Enough," my mother said, standing between us. "What is done, is," she reiterated, glaring at my father, who had also turned into his nightside creature. A taller, thicker version with dark claws and thick muscles. The beast always protected itself from threats. It did not care whether there were blood ties involved. Fathers killed sons, sons killed mothers, all in an effort to survive. "The ceremony with Serena is postponed but not canceled. We will still get an heir."

Father scoffed. "For what purpose if he's been tainted? It's all for naught."

"Not with Zane," she said and turned to the second in line.

Xcian.

"Fuck no. You are not going to pawn her off brother to brother. I forbid it." I'd never spoken up against my mother, but I would with this.

"She is the one the pantheon has chosen. She carries the perfect strain. This is no longer your choice."

"She is betrothed to me. It gives me power over her."

"If time is what you are asking, then you have it. The betrothal is only valid insofar that you are able to put an heir into her. You can no longer carry an heir because you no longer own your soul or your flame. This must fall on your brother." She turned to Xcian.

This was so royally fucked up.

Xcian was the first to walk away. The others followed suit. I retreated to the basement where they had secured Eric. Being in the same room with him was both exhilarating and toxic. I wanted to take him in the worst possible ways.

I pushed the door open, and my heart sank to my knees. Eric lay curled on his side on the small cot, trembling in the cold. No blanket to keep him warm, only the dirty clothes he'd worn for the ceremony. Dark pants, dark tunic, and boots. The chain circled his ankle, over the boot, and fastened to the iron anchor bolted to the cement floor. We only used the room when one of our demons needed to be secured. The chain's length gave him enough movement to use the bathroom and stay in bed, but nothing else.

While I understood my father's predisposition to assume the worst and see Eric as a threat, I knew it was wrong. Eric had disappeared during the ceremony. While his physical form remained on this plane, his mind had slipped into the aether. I'm sure he'd seen the construct I'd erected to keep my demons at bay and the center of my soul, which was *him*. My light, my darkness, Eric filled every inch of me. He'd shared his pain, his fear, the blame, and something warm that coated my insides. Something good. Could it have been love? As his emotions escalated, my pains lessened until all I felt was him. Us.

For one exhilarating moment, a blissful silence fell over the world around me. No evil occupied my soul, no pulsing waves in my mind, or cries at the edge of sound. The pressure inside of me had lifted, taking with it my own pain. It was at that moment that I knew my spirit had chosen Eric to share in my burden. And Eric had decided to accept it. Accept me.

The purity of it all was shattered by the chaos that followed.

Demons ripped out of their cages as I stood vulnerable. The Sentinel's power to keep them imprisoned was the main reason only a handful of them escaped and not the thousands. After everything, he'd stormed off with some choice words for my family. I didn't think he'd come back for Xcian's ceremony.

Eric had still been knocked out when we reached the mansion.

Serena and my mother were correct. I would never be bound to an heir, my child. My bloodline could continue with a human surrogate, but the child would never carry my demons, my power. The child would begin life with a clean slate.

My heart lifted at the thought. It was what I had always wanted. But would Eric want to share that life with me? Would he want another child? Would he hate me when he found out he would have to watch his sons die of old age while he remained behind?

That conversation would have to be shelved for later. He had enough to hate me for already.

I unlocked the chain around his ankle with the key I had lifted from my father and slipped behind him.

Elle Arroyo

Instinctively, he leaned back into my warmth, fitting perfectly against me. I cradled him as I had so long ago, inhaling the scent of iron and sulfur on his clothes. Evidence of where he'd gone to save me.

In my arms, everything felt right. At least for the few moments between night and day. Eric stirred and slowly broke through sleep. He didn't move, and I thought he'd shove me away. Perception of events was never as clear during the nightside hours as they were during the dayside. With his array of feelings, I couldn't pinpoint his mindset.

"What happens now?" he asked gently.

"You need to acclimate to our world. You'll be protected."

"I'd like to see my son."

"Of course." I didn't move, aware of every bodily contact. Even clothed, I sensed his desire, his needs. So damn tempting.

"Zane," he whispered, "I never meant for this to happen. You have to believe me."

"I do," I said quickly, although the sound of regret in his voice made me hurt inside. "I believe you."

He let out a relieved sigh that cut through my heart. "It was you." His voice only above a whisper. "That night, when Layla left me, it was you."

I drew him tighter into me, unable to find words to match what I felt.

"Can you promise me something?" he asked innocently.

"Vows are honored in blood, Eric. What are you asking?" I wanted to turn him on his back to look at his face but didn't want to break our seal.

He cleared his throat. "Can you promise me that

you'll do everything in your power to protect my sons? I can't—I won't be able to live with myself if anything happens to them."

I took a moment to push away the snickering demons in my mind telling me to end his sons. They were competing for my affection, and I did not play well with risk. I also couldn't lie to him and tell him everything was going to be okay when it wasn't. "If it is in my power, I will protect them. But death wears many faces, Eric. They will die one day." I let that sink in.

"I know," he finally whispered, peeling himself out of my arms and getting out of bed. "Maybe you can explain what's going on after you take me to see my son like you promised."

Knowing he'd run as soon as an opportunity presented itself, the controlling version of myself wanted to lock him up. Keep him in chains. Protected from everyone, even himself. But I had made a vow to protect them after the ceremony. And I couldn't break it. "Okay. I'll take you to Sebastian and you let me protect you. We'll figure the rest out."

Eric had no clue how much control he actually had over me. If he did, he'd order me to do things against my nature. Knowing my demons existed, I feared he'd order me to leave him the fuck alone, and I wasn't sure I could do that. Even if it meant the demons inside consuming me. Even if it meant ending the fucking world.

When his eyes lowered to take me in, my cock hardened. His primal need hit me like an electrical charge, lethal. Slowly, I narrowed the gap between us. He didn't move away, didn't fear me or flinch. My eyes traced the delicate features of his face and swept down to the column of his throat. A small shiver passed through him as I cupped his neck. "I'm sorry, Eric. I never meant to hurt you." My fingertips felt the intricate movement of his Adam's apple as he swallowed.

"I know," he said. "I believe you."

I almost asked how? Why? He shouldn't believe me.

"And I want to know everything. But not here."

Everything. The time had come for no more lies between us. I nodded. With him in tow, we silently walked out of the basement. The house, silent in sleep. I had no idea where my brother had stashed the kid and found him in his bedroom. He sharply opened the door, hovering over the doorway. His expression, dangerous. He had every right to be pissed at me. I just ruined his damn life. A whiff of booze and flowers hit me.

"What?" he hissed out before I could identify what smelled familiar.

"I'm taking him to his son. Are you coming?"

Xcian dragged his eyes over my shoulder to Eric, grinding his teeth, his jaw flexing. My brother wasn't as tall as me, none of them were, but he was a solid six foot four inches and built with solid muscle. "Give me a minute," he snapped and slammed the door on my face.

And the fucker had no respect.

I took Eric to my bedroom. While my mother preferred archaic furniture, my bedroom was more modern, with grays and sharp reds to contrast the dark. Eric seemed so out of place in it. He preferred the bucolic life. Small towns, small spaces. I shoved some articles of clothing in a duffel, figuring I'd have to purchase Eric some clothes later.

"Do you have my phone?" he asked.

"No. I'll get you one later."

He said nothing as we met Bennett and Xcian at the SUV. I preferred Bennett to have my back, but I needed him to protect Serena. Her family had sold her for this purpose. My mother would make sure she'd get an heir one way or another and until Hawke pulled his head out of his ass, I wasn't letting the fight go. It'd be Serena's choice. Fuck everything else. Xcian climbed into the driver's seat after sneering my way. He looked as if he'd literally crawled out of a hole in the wall. My brother had fucked through half the women population in the Americas throughout the centuries. Pheromones clung to him like sap on a tree. He'd probably banged a damn staff member. At least he'd taken a quick shower, his hair still wet.

"Stay with her," I told Bennett. "Under my orders. Call me if you need anything. I should be back within the week."

He nodded but I knew he didn't like it. I appreciated that he didn't argue.

I climbed into the car beside Eric and Xcian drove us out of the city.

Eric kept his eyes out the side window, lost in thought. Restraining the urge to reach out and assure him that I would keep him and his children safe, I turned away too.

We were an hour into the drive when his fingers slid over my hand. A ghost sensation traveled up my arm at the contact. Turning my hand, we were now palm to palm, interlacing our fingers together. The simple touch made me realize how different we were. My fingers were long and soft while his were calloused.

I'd retained my physical youth having stopped aging when I ascended at twenty-five, while he was seventeen years my senior. He'd no longer age now that we were bonded. In time, he'd learn what that meant, and I hoped he'd be kinder to me than I had been to Finnegan. My past always tainted my present. Taking responsibility for the consequences of my actions included what I'd done to the wraith. Having experienced my own bonding, I too would've probably gone insane had Eric denied me. Bringing about the end of the world in the process. What did that make me? Pure evil?

Although I would never hurt Eric like Finn had hurt me, I could understand why he'd betrayed me to Lucifer. Madness was an incipient thing. And Finnegan had a millennium to develop it.

"How much longer?" Eric asked, breaking me from my thoughts.

"An hour at most," I responded.

Xcian had said nothing in the past few hours.

"Is Sebastian okay?" he asked with a father's worry.

"He is."

"You don't understand, Zane. Sebastian, he's different." I hooked onto the pain in his voice. Trapped in the car, I could do nothing but listen. I also noticed Xcian sending Eric furtive glances from the rearview mirror, and that made me defensive. "I just need you to promise to keep us safe. He can't lose me, and I can't...I can't lose him."

I didn't speak, knowing that Eric needed to get something off his chest.

"You don't know what I've done," he said, still

looking out the window. His beautiful, sad profile illuminated in the dim light. "I'm a weak fool who doesn't deserve a happy ending for what I've done to him." I squeezed his hand, offering strength through our connection after feeling his pain. "Sebastian has always been hypersensitive. He feels everything exponentially. He's sweet, funny, and has a deep-rooted kindness, of all things. It makes him vulnerable. He trusts sometimes when he shouldn't. He believes all things to be inherently good."

I heard Xcian squeeze the steering wheel hard and noticed the tension on his shoulders, but he remained silent. I wasn't sure what the hell that meant.

"I stained that goodness in him after I"—a sob broke out of his lips—"after I tried to kill myself."

My chest felt as though someone had just slammed it with a bat. That I had left him in that state. That I had simply taken the coward's way. I could've lost him five years ago. Lost him permanently.

"I-I couldn't eat. I couldn't sleep. I lost my job, was on the verge of losing the house. Everything I built. Alejandro had gotten into trouble at school. A fight. Sebastian was always locked in his room. He'd gone silent for so long. My family was broken." He let out another sob and wiped his face. "I thought the boys would be better off with her. With me out of the picture, she'd come back for them. Be a mother again. I found a rope, went into the garage, and tied the noose off a beam. I got on a step stool and jumped. No suicide note. What was I going to write? Sorry for being a fuck-up. Sorry for turning your world inside out. Sorry for forcing your mother to fall out of love with me and leave. I had no voice."

He turned to me, eyes red, and his face wet with tears. "The beam broke, but I had already passed out. Sebastian found me, Zane. My little boy found me with the noose around my neck in a failed attempt to kill myself." He hiccupped and the floodgates opened once more. I pulled him into my chest, where he clung to me like a desperate man. "He never asked me why and never brought it up again. Remained by my side as often as possible, sacrificing his time for me. After he got accepted to college, I sold the house. Left to live like a damn cross-country hobo so that he could *leave* for college. So he could find a life outside protecting me. *Me.* He'd never gotten a chance to live and now…now I've brought this down upon him." A shattering sob broke out of him, and he clung to me tighter.

It hadn't been Eric who brought this upon them. It had been *me* and he didn't even blame me. He blamed himself. That reality did not escape my notice. It made me cling to him tighter. Want him more. I kissed the top of his head. "It's going to be okay, Eric. I promise you. Everything's going to be okay."

Xcian cut me a glare through the rearview.

Yeah, keep bullshitting yourself. Nothing is ever going to be okay with Eric and his family ever again.

Chapter Twenty-Six

Eric

I wasn't sure how long it took to drain myself from the tears that tore through me. My only saving grace was the kind words Zane kept saying. The way he held me and drew lines up and down my arm. Back in that cell, I had planned out my escape. The only threat I'd encountered so far was Zane and his family. And, okay, I hadn't forgotten about that guy in Alejandro's house, but he'd been after Zane, not me. So my plan was pretty pathetic. Get out of the chains, gain some trust so that Zane would leave me and Sebastian alone, and then run like the devil was chasing us. Which, in this case, might be the truth. But then I had woken up with Zane next to me and felt protected and something like love through our bond. Running wasn't an option for me. Not anymore.

I hadn't meant to tell him about Sebastian. But something about our handholding had all my regret surfacing. I knew my son was hypersensitive when he was born. He absorbed other people's emotions. Like me, he suffered for it. Except Layla had been my shield against the world. And now Zane offered that same protection. Sebastian had only me. And I had completely failed to protect him.

We reached a narrow side road flanked by trees

with low-hanging branches that obscured the road and scraped against the roof of the car like a warning to stay away. The only light was the SUV's headlights, which Xcian had turned off as we approached a two-story log cabin. The overhead light on the porch was on and there stood Sebastian beside a large, beautiful white dog. Or at least I hoped it was a dog but looked more like a wolf.

"You've got to be fucking kidding me," Zane hissed out.

"He showed up. Don't fucking blame me," Xcian said right before he got out of the car. But the young man didn't approach the house. He whistled, tapped his thigh, and the dog shot to his feet, following him toward the back of the house, leaving Sebastian alone. I noticed my son watching the young man and the dog expectantly. The smile on my son's face as he took me in melted all the pent-up stress. He was alive. He looked well. Unhurt.

"Dad!" He sprinted toward me.

We hugged, cried, and laughed. My boy. Taller than me, I cupped the back of his head and forced him to lean into me so I could whisper in his ear, "Are you really okay?"

He nodded and his eyes once again found Xcian as he and the dog slipped inside the cabin. "Yeah. He's, um, been protecting me this whole time. What about you?"

Sebastian lifted his eyes behind me to Zane, who must've been approaching. Having been locked up, I wasn't sure if they had met. By Sebastian's reaction, I gauged they had not.

Zane carried his duffle over his shoulder with one

hand, the other he placed possessively on my lower back. The move indicative of our relationship. Fake or not, we were something. "Uh, Sebastian, this is Zane," I said. I'd already explained things to Sebastian, though they had been a lie I'd have to rectify. Or Zane would have to since he'd been the one to lie to me.

Sebastian didn't let go of my arm, despite Zane towering over me. I felt a slight tug of war between them. Both of them trying to protect me.

"Nice to meet you, Sebastian," Zane finally conceded and lowered his hand. "I hope your accommodations have been adequate. We should go inside."

I didn't miss the look Sebastian gave to the car as if already masterminding a plan of escape. I felt proud of my boy. We followed Zane inside, keeping a safe whispering distance between us.

"We should—"

"I know," I said before he could continue. "We will." He offered a gentle, comforting squeeze on my arm as we headed into the cabin.

Sebastian locked the door behind him and quickly looked out the window. I guessed it was a habit of having been chased and cooped up in the place. Then he turned off the outside light.

Xcian was in the kitchen preparing food while the wolf had sidled on the rug in the living room, ignoring us.

I wanted to be alone with Sebastian to talk freely to him. Zane seemed to notice. "You'll be sharing my room." A tingling sensation ran down my spine at those words.

"Go get comfortable, Dad," Sebastian said. "You

look like you slept in cat litter."

"Wow," I said, dryly. "Thanks"

Sebastian hugged me. Yeah, the kid was a hugger. "We're going to be okay," he whispered, giving me a much-needed reminder that he was stronger than I thought. Plopping down on the sofa, he turned on the television hanging on the wall. I watched for a moment as the dog got to his feet and climbed up after him, laying his big head on top of Sebastian's lap.

"Doofus," Xcian called from the kitchen. The dog lifted his head and snarled at the man. "Off the sofa. *Now.*"

Sebastian laughed. A warm laugh that tickled my heart. Then he cupped the dog's face, nuzzling into his nose. "He's a mean man, I know." He coddled the large dog that could easily rip his throat out. The dog seemed to agree and ignored Xcian, resting his head back onto Sebastian's lap.

"It's okay, Ex," Sebastian said. "He's good."

Xcian made a face that looked anything but good.

Zane touched my elbow. "Let's get you cleaned up."

I followed him up the stairs. "That's a dog, right? Not a flesh-eating wolf?" My voice cracked a little.

Zane chuckled. "He's a vegan."

I snorted. Yeah, as if.

I forgot how organically dark the woods could get at night until we reached our bedroom. Zane started to shove things in the drawer with the lights still off. Apparently, seeing in the dark was one of his attributes. Not being human. The shine in his eyes, two dots in the darkness. Stumbling my way inside, I flicked the light switch on. Going from dark to light didn't faze him while it made me squint. At least until my eyes adjusted to the light.

"I'd prefer my own room." I sounded like a petulant child and crossed my arms over my chest like one, too.

He slammed the last drawer shut and slowly—because I was starting to learn that he moved slower when he was pissed as if restraining the urge to strangle me—he turned. I lifted my chin in defiance and his eyes lowered to my lips, sending all kinds of heat flooding through my body. So much for trying to be intimidating.

"No," he finally said. "You're not getting your own room."

That was it. He dismissed me and headed into the ensuite bathroom. More sounds of things being moved as if he were searching for something, or ensuring I couldn't escape before he returned to the room. "Get undressed and clean up. You smell like shit." With that he strutted—yeah, strutted—out of the bedroom.

Asshole. I did stink. Once undressed, I walked naked into the bathroom. Even though I'd written three bestsellers that earned me more than a decent wage, I had never allowed myself the luxuries of living in large homes or using lavish showers larger than my last bedroom. My mother always told me to use my money because I couldn't take it with me to the grave, but I never wanted anything more than basic accommodations. Another reason why Layla left me.

The large stone shower had multiple sprays hitting my sensitive skin. The water cascaded down my head and body as I leaned forward, one hand on the wall. I had aged pretty well, in my honest opinion. I'd lost weight and built some definition from living a rugged life. Chopping wood, landscaping, taking long walks. Alone. A piece of me missing. I'd always thought it had been Layla. Replaying our lives together in my head, it hadn't been that we fit as a couple, but that she shielded me from life. I'd wrapped myself in her so completely, that it shattered me when she left me. I couldn't go through that again. I wouldn't survive it. Not with Zane. Was he even capable of loving me? Would he find a way to break our link so he could have a child with Serena? The thought hollowed me out, carved me into pieces.

The door to the bathroom creaked open, and without so much as permission, a very naked Zane walked in and climbed into the shower behind me.

Before I asked what the hell, he cupped my hip with one hand, pulling my ass into his erection as he snaked his other arm around my body and cupped my soft cock. The move scattered all thought of voicing any type of complaint. His hands made smooth motions up and down my shaft, getting it painfully hard as his cock slid up and down the crease of my ass. The thought of feeling him inside of me made me clench up. Wanting and fearing it. His lips grazed my ear.

"Don't doubt me, Eric." The vibration of his husky voice against my skin made me pliant against him. "I will never hurt you."

Never hurt me. Those words in need of being picked apart. Would he never hurt my feelings? Would he never hurt me physically? Would he keep my boys safe so I wouldn't be hurt? The questions scattered in my mind as he dipped his fingers under my balls, the friction of it making me bite back a moan. Thinking couldn't happen while he touched me. Leaning into his shoulder, I turned my head, searching out his mouth. The kiss. The beautiful kiss I so desperately needed. But he refused to give me what I wanted. Refused to budge. The raw need to control him rushed through me. Strength whipped through me and I had him pinned to the wall, his back to me.

I may not have had control over my life but fuck if I wouldn't have control over this.

God, the guy was massive. Every ounce of him, tight muscles and smooth flesh. He could fight me on this, reclaim control, but he didn't. I licked his throat and the whimper that passed his throat made me vibrate with anticipation.

"I choose how this plays out." He shuddered at my words. "Tell me yes, or we can stop this right now."

"Yes," he said, breathlessly.

I dropped to my knees, spread his cheeks, and gave him one slow lick along his crease. My intent clear. He pushed his ass back, leaning forward allowing me to spread him wider. Fuck, he had a nice ass. The small pucker tight. My position awkward despite the shower large enough for both of us. I gave him another lick, twirling my tongue deeper against his tight hole, loving the sounds he made as he melted with my touch. My limited knowledge of pleasuring someone this way notwithstanding, I went with it. Sucking the tight ring of muscle. Feeling every emotion coursing through his body. The bond. It had to be the bond.

"Fuck, yes, Eric. Please."

The begging drew on my own need to protect him. To give him what he needed. Scrambling to my feet, I grabbed the conditioner and squeezed a generous amount on my fingers, then pushed a finger inside his tight hole. He pushed back deeper, writhing. "More. Please fuck." Complying, I pushed in another, spreading him open. His body was so fucking tight. "Tell me you want me, Zane. Only me. I want to know that you will always be only mine." The alternative would break me.

He growled, reacting to my fingers. "Only you. Only fucking you," he said through gritted teeth.

Good enough for me.

I glazed my cock with the conditioner and guided it to his hole. Cupping his hips, I plunged into him, breaching the first tight ring of muscle, watching as his body swallowed me in one smooth glide. He brutally clung to my thighs, bruising me, marking me. I pulled out and slammed into him again. The wet slide so fucking hot. His body so fucking perfect. This man. My man. The one who already owned my heart. Fired up all my nerve endings. Our joined bodies only a piece of our union. A very important piece right now. I growled through the friction and hit that spot, forcing a deep moan out of him. Then his body started to shift, uncoiling into something else. Muscles tightened on his back, his skin turned a shade of gray, and he started to grow.

Anunnaki. Demon. All a part of him and they were all mine.

It lasted only a heartbeat. Stumbling back, I almost slipped, but he caught me with one massive arm and our mouths collided. He thrust his tongue inside with no hesitation. I opened for him, needing the desperate kiss. The kiss he'd given me only once, and that had shattered my very existence. I knew he'd done something to me with that first kiss. This one was just as chaotic. He sucked my tongue long and hard. Then nipped my lips before going back in to repeat it all over again. My fingers dug into his wet hair, trying to absorb the power emanating from his very soul through our lips. Fuck. I'd only ever kissed Layla and this, *this* was a thousand times better. This was transcendent. This was why people read romance novels. I'd never believed something as banal as a kiss could be extraordinary.

Somehow, we made it to the bed. I clung to him as he lowered me down, never breaking the kiss. His powerful body on mine as he slotted our cocks together, jerking his hips, seeking out a perfect rhythm. The friction drove me mad. I needed more. Wanted more. He trailed open-mouthed kisses to my pulse point and paused. "I'm so fucking sorry, Eric."

I loved that he used my name and not something as generic as babe or baby. I wanted him to know exactly who he was sharing this moment with. "I know," I said in a breathy whisper. I moaned as he rocked gently against me. "I want to be inside you, Zane." I knew I was being greedy and selfish, but I needed this.

He trailed kisses down my chest and nipped at my nipples before straddling my hips. I felt his long, thick shaft on my belly as he reached for the lube.

I swallowed the rising need to take control. His soft fingers lubing my cock felt like heaven. The chaos burned through and everything slowed. Everything became deliberate and not just about sex, but about us. His blue eyes met mine as he lifted himself over my erection. No words spoken between us, only our shared hunger for each other. Our connection held as he slowly, so damn slowly, lowered himself onto my cock, sucking a part of me inside his body. His eyes half-lidded. His lips met mine in a fervent kiss I would never tire to receive. He rode me hard, sweat gleaming against his skin. The scent of musk and rain overpowered everything else.

"Touch me," he breathed out.

And I did. He felt like velvet under my fingers as I stroked him. I must've hit the sweet spot because his body tensed, and he was riding me harder now. I chased the movement with him, my cock pulsing with oversensitivity at this point.

"I'm not going to last," I said. My balls tightened. Shit, fuck. "Not yet, Zane, please."

He quickly pulled his body away as if I'd scorched him. The loss of his nearness instantly sparked more need. The confused look on his face almost had me giggling like an idiot. I countered it with a savage kiss of my own. He hesitated a moment, before plunging his tongue inside my mouth, warring for control. He didn't have to be guided. He knew exactly where I wanted him. On his back, opened up for me. Dragging myself away from that hard kiss to see what belonged to me took a monumental effort. Running my hand down his chest, taking in all of him, made his stomach clench and his cock glistened, hard and red. His knees bent and spread open. At that moment, Zane's submission so damn erotic. Ready and waiting for me. His eyes never left my face. A pearl of cum glossed the tip of his cock and I licked my lips, wanting to taste him. Later. Definitely later. Right now I needed to be inside that perfect ass of his. Positioned between his legs, tearing my eyes from his body to see his reaction, I drove my cock into him hard. Arching his hips, he fisted the sheets at his side. I didn't stop, couldn't stop pummeling him into the mattress. My ass muscles contracted with every thrust. A sex-drunk Zane under me totally fucking hot.

"Eric," he hissed out, and I caught a glimpse of his fangs. Fangs! Nope. I wasn't going to let that distract me. "I'm going to come."

I plunged harder until he cried out. Cum shot out of his cock in pulsing waves that seemed never to stop. Still seeking my own release, I continued to thrust hard, deeper, all the way to my balls. Shaking the bed in the process and not giving a shit. His ass clenched down on my cock, painfully and deliciously. A cry tore out of me as my body jerked through the violent orgasm. It seemed to go on and on until I finally slumped on top of him, hiding my face in the crook of his neck, inhaling his heady scent. Again, this time there was a mixture of earth and musk on his skin and I wanted nothing more than to remain on him, breathing him in. Forever. The room suddenly grew silent, except for an echo of the television downstairs.

"Not to break the mood," Zane said, his voice dark and husky, "but I think they heard us downstairs."

Heat drifted from my neck to my scalp as I remembered Sebastian and Xcian. Zane laughed and hugged me tighter. I wanted to crawl away and die somewhere.

"You're my mate, Eric. Your son knows that now."

If he hadn't, he sure as hell did now. I slipped out of his body and he quickly drew me into his arms, kissing my forehead.

My mind swirled with all the intimate things we

hadn't done. Like dinner, a date, or a movie. Walking hand-in-hand along the lakefront. Then there were the intimate things he could teach me in bed. I kissed his chest and placed my hand over his heart. "Uh," I said, because I didn't know how to phrase what I wanted to say to him. "Fangs?" I felt his heart quicken under my palm.

"I'm not human, Eric. You haven't seen the monster inside of me."

There was a long pause as I felt his strong, beating heart. I should be afraid, but I wasn't. "Will the monster be sharing my bed too?" The question left my mouth before I had time to think.

"I'm the only monster you'll have in your bed," he growled out. "But not yet. I don't want to scare you tonight. This is new." He kissed my nose. His fangs were no longer visible. "I'll show you all of me soon."

I shuddered at the thought.

Chapter Twenty-Seven

Zane

Eric wanted to see my monster. He wasn't afraid of me, wasn't running from me. His kisses flooded me with heat. The only word I could use to describe the indescribable. He turned me into a submissive twink with those kisses. I had nothing against twinks. They were the most beautiful in the world. The light in the dark. The joy with the hateful. Which wasn't me. I didn't usually bottom. It gave me no control, and I needed control of everything except this. With Eric. I gave my control to him willingly. I'd give him the stars, the moon, the fucking ocean if he asked for it.

I cupped his face, sliding my fingers into his hair to see him better. His brown eyes captured mine in hunger. Then he turned his head and kissed my palm, before trailing kisses lower, hesitantly. I knew he was new at being with a man and it showed in the way he explored me with his mouth.

"Eric," I said as he kissed me just under my pelvis. "You don't have to."

"Do you want me to?" he asked with a slight edge to his tone.

"Fuck, yes," I said, and my cock responded by pulsing in its erection.

I watched Eric as he gave me one slow, tentative

lick underneath from the base to tip, licking off my slit. Then he smiled. A smile that seemed to light up the world in its sincerity. His eyes lit with flame, and something other than just bodily lust or hunger. The look he'd given me after my squeal in the shower when he'd first caught me naked. A mixture of sweet embarrassment and curiosity. At least right before Bennett had ruined it.

"You like that?" he asked.

"You know I do," I said, palming my shit and lifting my hips to my own touch. He smacked my hand away.

"No touchy."

Hellfire, help me. This man would end me with a simple smile. He licked his plump lips and opened his mouth to take me all in. And demon be damned, the heat of his mouth had all my nerve endings firing at once. I dropped my head on the pillow, unable to watch him for fear I'd prematurely explode. At first, he sucked nervously, then he went all out, taking me to the back of his throat. I jerked deeper and he pulled sharply away. "Shit, Eric, sorry."

"I can't take you all."

"It's okay, whatever you do feels good."

Damn, that man blushed. Not that he'd give up on testing the waters—he seamed his lips over my tip and sucked slowly. Cool hands wrapped around my base and I shuddered at the contact. More so when he started to pump me, running the tip across his lips, licking, sucking. Driving me insane. I dug my hand into his hair, and he moaned. The vibration of the sound went straight up my cock and into my spine, branching out to every cell in my body. Seconds away from blowing my load, I bit down on my lip to keep the moan in check.

"Eric, I'm gonna come."

That made him suck harder, faster, until my hips jerked into his mouth, forcing him to gag just as I blew. My body stiffened, then went pliant as he swallowed my cum. When he pulled away, his lips and chin were wet with me. My seed. My juices. *Mine.* Before he could attempt to wipe it, I lifted him flush against my body, slamming my mouth against his. He stiffened slightly but melted into my need quickly. We were a heady mix, and I loved every fucking second of it. We warred with our tongues, taking equal control of the kiss.

He was *mine*.

I stopped him from pulling away and gave him one good clean lick before releasing him. "Fuck, you are dirty."

"Me? You did pretty well yourself."

He smirked and wiped his mouth. "I think I need another shower."

"I'll join you," I said.

He pushed me back onto the bed before I could rise. "No. I really need to shower and get downstairs to Sebastian."

"And?"

"And," he said, leaning into my neck and giving me a slow lick. "I don't need more temptation from you."

Before I could say anything, he jumped off the bed and slipped into the bathroom. This time, I heard the door lock. Yeah, I could break the shit and join him. But I figured maybe he deserved some space. Especially with what I meant to tell him.

After my shower, I dressed and met Eric, Sebastian, and Xcian downstairs. Eric was sitting in the armchair rigidly, watching a newscast, but I knew he wasn't paying attention to it. What he was paying attention to was Sebastian lying on the sofa asleep with his head on Xcian's lap as my brother played with the kid's hair. A gentle move coming from my very obnoxious, violent brother. The scene too endearing to disturb. I figured that was the reason Eric hadn't gone ballistic and forced them apart. Not that Xcian looked like anyone could move him.

"Xcian, we have to talk," I said.

Doofus lifted his head and cocked it. I glared at him, and he whimpered, lowering his head again. I ignored the wrenching feeling in my gut to get Doofus away from us and back home where he belonged. He seemed to notice my intent and yipped at the air, then growled low. That's when Sebastian stirred, sat up with his hair muffled, and rubbed his eyes. The kid looked like his father. So much so, it was hard to pick them apart. Except for the age difference and their hairstyles. Sebastian had his hair much longer and straighter.

"Oh," he said. Realizing that he'd fallen asleep on Xcian's lap, he slid to the other side of the sofa, as far away from my brother as he could get. "Uh, what's going on?"

Xcian took that moment to get to his feet and turn off the television. He remained standing by it, though. I believed if he could, he would have preferred to be farther away from the boy who looked so innocent and young, blinking away the sleep that still clung to him. My emotions for the boy were still a swirl of confusion. Eric's sons were now mine. They were part of his blood, and I was part of him. This shit was going to be harder than I thought.

I took the seat Xcian vacated as both humans watched me. "Time for truths."

"Zane, once you do this, there is no going back."

I knew that. "It's too late to go back. For any of you." I looked at Eric and then Sebastian, before eyeing Xcian. Although my brother wasn't in agreement with my decision, he didn't stop me either. "As you may have guessed, my family and I are not necessarily human. We have walked the earth for millennia, cursed in our immortality to live among you. Our original charge was to protect the human race. To ensure a balance of the threats inherent in such a young world. We are at war against what we call the malice. A group of beings with the ability to mimic humans. They live among you but are seeking to destroy us and take back what they believe belongs to them." I waited for at least the kid to bust out laughing, or crying, or both. When nothing happened, I suspected Xcian must've already ratted us out. I'd file that for later and continued. "We've harvested the powers of the demons we've imprisoned in order to protect this world." I took in Eric's stoic expression, though his eyes were very much expressive. I just didn't know if he thought I needed medication, or he needed therapy.

"Who's Finn?" Eric finally asked, and anger writhed through me. A powerful force that wanted out. "I, uh, I think I may have gone to the ethereal place, and he was there. Said something about Hell and Lucifer."

Xcian grunted, and I had to restrain the urge to growl.

Elle Arroyo

"Finnegan is a wraith, born of Lucifer. Yes, the Lucifer of Hell. Not an angel, but an immortal asshole who is arrogant and evil in every way."

"Finn said that Lucifer wanted you back. What does that mean?"

"It means nothing," I said, ignoring Xcian's rising anger that smelled of smoke. My brothers didn't know the extent of my torture under Lucifer. If they did, they would rebel, and that would be bad. *Really* bad. "Lucifer cannot force me back. And he's not taking anyone I care about." Not again.

Doofus whimpered again. Sebastian quickly got to his feet and dropped beside the animal, lulling him to submission. I could tell Xcian had a problem with that, but my brother remained silent. I should've sent Doofus home, but I didn't think Leander would appreciate being called out as a wolf shifter in front of the humans. And I didn't want to make things any worse than they already were with my explanations. It was one thing to explain about my kind, another to explain about demons, shifters, vampires, and other things that lived in the night.

"Every one of your brothers has a demon inside them?" Sebastian asked.

"Not all of us. We ascend during our mid-twenties in human years. Three of us are still underage."

"How old are you?" Eric asked.

"Old."

"How old."

"Thousand, give or take."

Yeah, the expression Eric wore was expected. I knew he wanted to ask more questions about how everything affected him, but not in front of Sebastian. It

208

gave me time to come up with answers I didn't have.

"This malice thing. These people. They were the ones at Alex's house?" Sebastian asked, looking at me over his shoulder. "Looking for *you*."

"Yes. They will try to use whatever they can to get to me."

"Why you?" Sebastian asked. "What makes *you* so special?"

The clipped tone in his voice made it perfectly clear Sebastian did not approve of me. I hadn't earned it yet. "I'm the oldest. I carry some of the strongest demons inside me. Killing me would set them free."

Sebastian turned back to focus on the wolf. He said nothing after that, which confirmed that something happened between Xcian and him that had Sebastian already aware of the world he'd entered. I sent a glare to Xcian, which he returned tenfold.

Eric finally leaned forward. "Zane," he said. "You know we can't just stay prisoners here."

"Haven't you heard anything?" Xcian hissed out. "You leave our protection, you die. How long do you think it'll take a malice to peel the flesh from your bones?"

"Xcian," I scolded.

"Or do worse to your sons?"

Eric got to his feet. "This is a lot to take in. I'd like to speak with my son. Alone."

Xcian stepped forward as if he meant to bowl right over Eric. "You are the reason we are all in this fucking mess!"

I jumped to my feet, stepping between them. Sebastian followed too, and so did Doofus. Xcian's eyes burned with hellfire. Fuck. "Xcian, stop it." But it was too late. Xcian lunged at Eric. I interceded, slamming into Xcian, knocking him where Sebastian had been standing just moments before.

Xcian punched me in the face. His muscles shifted underneath his skin. His demon rising to the surface. Something that shouldn't have happened if he were in control. I slammed him a few times, my own shift close until we were nothing but a tangle of limbs, breaking shit in our path. I tried to hold him back, and he tried to chase Eric. My body morphed into my true self, coated in thick skin, taller, bulkier, and eyes glowing red.

The last thing I saw was Eric snatching the car keys I'd left on top of the counter, grabbing Sebastian's hand, and running out of the cabin. Doofus jumped to his feet and ran out with the father-son duo.

Eric was gone. He'd left me.

Chapter Twenty-Eight

Eric

"Doofus!" Sebastian cried out to the dog waiting at the door.

I didn't have the heart to leave the animal behind since it clearly wanted to get away from the brothers' fight to the death. Sebastian opened the door so the dog could climb inside, and I stepped on the gas, forcing the SUV into a slide before straightening it and zooming down the narrow blacktop, flicking on the headlights so we wouldn't end up wrapped around a tree. I swerved right onto the main road and took a chance to glance at the rearview mirror, half-expecting something to chase us. Something with four legs and large teeth. Fangs. God, Zane had fangs. I had ignored it in the throes of passion, but I saw what he'd become to protect me from his brother.

"I don't understand," Sebastian said beside me. The dog had jumped into the back seat. "Why would he attack you? That's not him. That's not."

I wasn't sure if Sebastian was trying to convince me or himself. Probably both. "We don't know what they are, Seba," I said, trying to sound calmer than I felt. "We can't know if anything they told us is real or if they're just…"

"Monsters," he whispered.

He turned his head to look out the window, and I knew he'd felt something for the young man that had saved his life back at the house. I couldn't very well try to convince him of the millions of reasons why having any concern for him was a bad idea since I felt torn for just leaving Zane behind. But surely, his brother wouldn't kill him.

"They'll be fine," I finally said. "They're brothers. Brothers fight. How many times have you and Alejandro fought?"

"Never, Dad. Alejandro would kill me in a fight."

True. "Didn't stop him from arguing with you, though."

"That wasn't an argument back there."

No. It wasn't, so I kept my mouth closed.

"We have to get Alejandro before they find him," Sebastian said.

"I know." I didn't tell Sebastian that they were already watching Alejandro. That Zane had used their safety to manipulate me into whatever crazy ritual had me guilty for leaving him. That had to be the reason why I felt my chest about to cave. Why my fingers itched to turn the car around and return to him. The pull was too damn strong to be anything other than a spell. Love wasn't all-consuming. Love wasn't debilitating. Not the love I'd ever experienced before. This was something else. This was *more*. This was our tether. The binding. Not real feelings. The farther I got away, the clearer my thoughts became. I'd been so stupid. So damn stupid.

My dad used to tell stories about my grandfather being some kind of witch in the mountains of Puerto Rico. Not a *curandero* type witch, more like a witch who performed spells and rituals that made people do things. One night when my father was drunk, he told me he had many brothers and sisters he'd never met because my grandfather cheated on my grandmother, and he had the *hechizos* to make women fall in love with him. Some sort of love spell.

Doofus whimpered.

Believing Zane was some sort of immortal, sex god that had put a spell on me to fall in love with him made more sense than me actually falling in love with the man who lied to me about who he was, threatened my kids, and forced me into some sort of satanic ritual to bind himself to me, right?

"Dad?"

I snapped out of my thoughts. "Yeah?"

"How the hell are we going to get to New York? I have no ID or phone on me. Do you?"

Fuck. They had completely stripped me of everything. Even my phone. I thought about our possible plan with no ID. It'd take forty-two hours driving cross-country to New York. And no money in my pocket. No ID, no way to buy a phone, a car, or a plane ticket. I had my money in the damn bank and, without a valid ID, we were up shit creek. I'd never planned for this just-in-case scenario. Which meant that we had to go to the one person I swore never to *ever* ask anything from. "Is your mother still in the city?"

Sebastian looked about ready to vomit and he leaned back. "Yeah."

"She can pull money from my account. Enough to buy a phone and a plane ticket so I can go get your brother."

"*We*, Dad. You are not leaving me with her."

I ran my hand down my face. I smelled of Zane's soap with a whiff of him still. "I think you should stay with her."

"No," Sebastian said thickly. "You leave me with her, and I'll run."

I turned to him. "This isn't a game. Xcian was right. You should've stayed with him back in the cabin. He'll protect you."

I wished I hadn't said that because Sebastian opened the door. I grabbed his sleeve before he could jump out of a moving car and turned into the shoulder, stopping the SUV with a jolt before releasing him. He jumped out, leaving the door open, and Doofus followed protectively behind him. I jumped out of the car already swallowing back tears. If that fucker hurt my son, I'd kill him. I didn't care. "Seba!"

He dropped on all fours. His long, inky black hair covered his face. I didn't dare touch him, but I dropped beside him, watching as he fisted the dirt under him. His hands opened and closed as the coarse dirt sifted through his fingers. Something he always did when he'd been on the verge of a panic attack. As if the feel of the ground soothed him. "No one can protect us, Dad. Not Xcian, not Zane. If we can't do this ourselves, we're dead men." He shook his head. "You didn't see those men when they broke into the house. They weren't men. You didn't see…" He didn't offer anything else though I wanted to ask what he'd seen that had terrified him like this. What had they done to him? I didn't dare dredge it all up again. Not here, not when we were still running.

"Okay. We do this together then."

He nodded. "Together."

214

Doofus scrambled toward us and started licking Seba's face. My son laughed and hugged the animal close. I laughed too and petted the freaky wolf-dog. "We should find another name for him. I don't think Doofus fits."

That got Seba laughing harder as if in on an inside joke I was not privy to. A moment passed before starting toward the truck.

After driving a couple of hours, the sun started to rise in the sky. We parked the SUV in a part of the city where it wouldn't be found for days. Searching through the SUV, we found a couple of hundred dollars, a first aid kit, some large clothes, and a service pack for Doofus.

We made it to the Luxe Hotel before the sun was high in the sky and spent a couple of hours watching the place for anything resembling the Crawford brothers. "I think we're good," Sebastian said. Then he turned to Doofus. "We're good, right?"

The wolf-dog didn't answer. With no other choice, we walked into the lobby of the hotel.

"Excuse me, sir, but animals are not allowed."

I turned to the young clerk. "He's a service animal," I said. "And we're only visiting. You wouldn't take someone's eyeballs out, would you?" I hissed out, speaking louder and getting more attention than I hoped. Sebastian took the hint and acted blind.

"Dad, Dad, where are you?" His voice trembled, hands out to the air. A bit of overkill but whatever. We were desperate.

"What room?" the woman asked.

Sebastian gave her the number and she called Layla. After confirming who we were, she allowed us to go upstairs with a note to security about our quick departure.

Doofus was a large dog but well-behaved. He remained next to Seba, and I knew the dog wasn't all as he appeared. There was a knowing gaze in his eyes. He turned to look at me and chills ran through me. Those eyes weren't dog. They weren't wolf. They almost looked human.

Thankfully, the elevator door opened, and Sebastian started for his mother's room. It wasn't Layla who opened the door to greet us. Or scowl at me. Alejandro swung the door open with a pissed-off look. Alejandro was all Layla. Warm blond hair, and deep-set hazel eyes, touching on green. He stood taller than Sebastian and like his mother, he perfected the scowl, which was what he was wearing right now.

"Where the fuck have you been?" he snapped at Sebastian.

Unable to restrain himself, Sebastian launched himself at Alejandro and hugged him tightly. "You're okay," I heard my son say.

"Me?" Alejandro returned into Sebastian's ear. "I was so fucking worried about you."

"Can we, uh, come inside," I interrupted.

They parted and Alejandro opened the door wider, eyeing the dog. "I'm allergic, you know that, right?"

I walked into the spacious room. Something Layla and I had never afforded before. When we'd gone on vacations with the boys, we always drove, and always stayed in economy-priced places, which meant smelly rugs and coarse towels. Not like this place that actually had a terrace. Apparently, Alejandro had received a call from the cops regarding the break-in at the house. It had been a courtesy call because the owner had mentioned that he hadn't left the keys before he vacated. That had been Sebastian's responsibility. So when Sebastian hadn't answered Alejandro's calls, and I didn't answer, Alejandro had hopped on a plane back to LA.

After hugging Sebastian, I expected Layla to hit me with a verbal onslaught on how irresponsible I was not to have called. But instead, she wrapped her arms around my neck and hugged me tightly. "You jerk," she said into my ear, so only I heard. "You scared us."

I felt nothing for the woman holding me. Not the slightest pull when she'd loved me. Not my heart sinking a little bit every time she walked away. I missed Zane's touch. I missed Zane. "I messed up, Layla. Big time," I admitted to her.

Her hand cupped the back of my head. "We'll figure it out. We always do."

I wanted to believe her. I just didn't think this would be so easy to figure out. At least not where we could survive this.

I let her lead me to the balcony where Pedro waited. Her smile brightened as she pulled away from me to kiss him. Although we'd managed to remain civil around the boys, attending special events and birthdays together as a blended family, I'd never really looked at Layla when she'd been coddling Pedro. I did now, and she looked radiant. In love. I'd never really thought about her feelings for him before. I only saw how she'd hurt me. How she discarded me like a piece of shit and abandoned her kids. But watching her truly in love didn't leave that resentment inside of me like it used to. It didn't leave a fit of toxic jealousy, either. I felt happy for her. I wanted what they had so how could I be a hypocrite and curse what she had with Pedro? How could their love be wrong when it was true?

True.

Real.

The things I didn't have with Zane, though I had wanted so badly.

"Doofus?" Sebastian said.

I heard the dog growling, snapping me out of my revelation and back to the present. Doofus seemed to have stretched bigger when he saw Pedro. No longer a dog, but a wolf. Then he started to growl.

"Sebastian, that thing shouldn't be here," Layla said, waving at the wolf whose whole fur suddenly stood on end, staring at Pedro.

Alejandro quickly took his mother's hand and led her behind him. Somehow, Alejandro knew something was wrong too.

"Put your wolf away, son," Pedro said.

Pedro took a step closer to Alejandro as if intending to cower behind my son.

Layla struggled against Alejandro's hold. "Let me go, Alejandro. What in God's name is going on?"

Two things happened at that exact moment.

The room's door exploded inward, and Pedro lunged for Layla. Alejandro shoved his mother out of the way. Pedro rammed into him instead, and Doofus pounced on them. The trio scrambled back, dangerously close to the edge in a tangle of limbs. I reached for Alejandro, already seeing the inevitable. Too late.

They disappeared over the railing.

Sebastian stood frozen in time. Layla screamed. And I jumped after them.

Chapter Twenty-Nine

Zane

My hands curled into tight fists as I imagined how her delicate neck would feel as I crushed it.

"Calm the fuck down, Zane," Bennett ordered.

There weren't many options for Eric if he were going to get to New York. And we had already known Alejandro was in LA with his mother. Someone, possibly a fucking malice, had called him in New York to let him know about the apartment. It hadn't been the landlord. That fat ass was found dead in his house from a heart attack the day after we cleaned up the house.

We were in the adjacent room to Layla's and my brother, Noah, had inserted a camera feed that gave us a good look of Layla hugging Eric. Eric melted into her touch, and I hated her instantly. I growled and sneered at Xcian, who I was still pissed at. The reason we hadn't busted into the room had been because of Leander. AKA Doofus. My younger brother, the shifter, had inserted himself into Sebastian's good graces. Their connection had been genuine. People usually stayed away from the wolf version of my brother. Not Sebastian. The boy had instantly sensed the kindness in the animal. In Leander. Something I asserted to be due to his hypersensitivities. Just like his father. Only if Eric would give into those feelings and trust himself the

Elle Arroyo

way his son did, things would go so much easier for him. Like maybe he wouldn't fucking run from me.

At least with Leander with them, the wolf would be able to sense the malice when they showed up because this little family reunion was a fucking trap.

"Have the teams checked in?" I asked.

We had a total of six teams watching the area. Four-man teams meant twenty trained men, including my brothers and Bennett, casing the place for threats. "Yes, all have checked in, and still nothing."

Xcian sighed. "Maybe they don't care about your lover, Zane. Maybe he's safe without you."

That hurt because I was starting to wonder the same thing.

At least until we heard Leander begin to growl.

Everything after that happened too fast.

Xcian and I were the first busting through the door just as Leander and Alejandro fell over. Then Eric leapt. Time slowed as my body moved, catching Eric before he cleared the railing. I pulled him back and over hard enough to send us both sprawling on our backs. He screamed his son's name, fighting against my hold.

All I saw was Leander, the portal opening, and the trio disappeared.

Eric elbowed my ribs and jumped to his feet. I caught him at the railing as he looked down. They were gone, not splattered on the pavement. Gone. Eric shook his head. "I don't understand. Where, where did they go?"

I didn't have time to explain things. Not here. "We are out of here. Now," I ordered, pulling in the need to follow the trio into Hell.

Eric ripped his arm out of my grasp. "I'm not

leaving without him!" The desperate sound of his voice almost tore me in half.

I would've given anything to change the past at that moment. To give Eric back his cozy little life in Maine, chasing moose and fighting ladybugs. "He's alive," I said. Then to Xcian, who had turned three shades paler than usual. "We're retreating to the safehouse."

"What about Leander?" Hawke asked. "We can't just leave him."

"We won't, but we can't do shit from here."

Eric yanked his hand away from me and dropped to Layla's side. He touched her cheek, and I swore I wanted to cage her somewhere far away.

"Layla, baby, Alejandro is alive."

Her eyes were wide, her lips trembling. "I don't understand. Pedro, why would he? Where's Alejandro?"

"Eric," I snapped. "We have to go now. More will come."

"I'm not leaving her."

Galen bristled. Had it been his decision, he would've put a bullet in both their heads. Easy clean-up. "Then bring her," I snapped.

"Layla, come on. We'll figure it out later." Eric's gentle voice soothed his ex while my insides screamed.

Thankfully, I had damage control to worry about, and that meant Noah had taken the lead. I heard him spewing orders into the radio to inform the other teams of our intent to evacuate the building. We still had to climb down twenty floors and hope that Pedro had been the only malice injected before we started surveilling the place. Which was not likely.

"We go in sets of four," Noah said over the noise.

Eric had Layla's hand in his while the other cupped the back of Sebastian's neck in a hug. Sebastian visibly sobbing for his brother. "I'll make this right, Seba. I promise." I could tell Eric was warring with the decision of leaving his little family, which made me realize I wasn't in that group. He'd discarded me the moment he ran from me to his ex. Once I got that fucking clear in my head, I could move on. I could make adjustments and survive. I wasn't the first asshole to lose his soul to someone who didn't give a shit about him. That was the luck of the draw. Fucking fate.

"I need you to get them out of here. Get them to safety," I said to Noah.

Noah squeezed my shoulder. "I will."

"I have to go after Leander."

"I know," he said.

"I'm coming with you," I heard Eric to my left. Layla and Sebastian stood watching. Xcian looked about ready to jump out of the balcony to test fate, and Galen had his hand too close to his holster at his hip.

"I'm sorry, Mr. Diaz, but no. You can't," Noah said kindly.

Eric seemed taken aback by the kindness in his tone but recovered quickly and scowled. "I'm getting my son back and you,"—he shoved his finger into my chest—"Are going to help me because you,"—another poke—"promised to keep them safe."

One collective gasp went through the room, and the silence burned my ears. "If you would've remained under my protection," I countered, "you would've been safe, and the malice would not have shown his colors."

"If you hadn't put some sort of spell on me in the

first place, I wouldn't have been in this mess!"

Now it was my turn to figure out the workings of the human mind. "Spell? What fucking spell?"

"You put a spell on me so that I'd fall in love with you, asshole! And I want it gone! Gone! Because I don't want this. I don't want to be in love with you." Another poke.

I died and went to Hell. Right there. Until Hawke started to laugh, then masked it with a cough when I shot him a death glare. I narrowed the gap between Eric and me, ignoring the probing eyes of my family and his listening in. "What spell do you think I placed over you?" Because there was no fucking spell to force someone to fall in love with you. Every broken-hearted sap had searched and found nothing.

Eric's eyes landed on mine with nothing but stubborn pride. "This feeling that I have for you. It's…it's not real." He sounded less sure of himself.

"What feeling?"

He rubbed his chest, unaware that he was doing it. "Like I'd die if something happens to you. Like I want to hold you constantly. Like wondering what your favorite color is and if you'd enjoy a walk along the waterfront holding hands. Or if you prefer chocolate or vanilla ice cream and if you'd ever consider volunteering at the library to read with the kids there. I want to know what it would feel like falling asleep in your arms and waking up in the morning with you." He shook his head as if coming out of a haze. "None of it makes sense."

Everything suddenly did make sense. To me. Eric loved me. *Eric loved me*.

"Eric," Layla said. "Are you *gay*?"

And that snapped Eric out of whatever reverie he'd been captured in. He scowled. "No. Because this was never real."

"Dad."

Something passed between father-son in that brief look between them that gave Eric purpose and he turned back to me with determination in his eyes. "I'm going with you to get my son."

I grabbed his hand, ignoring the surge of electricity shooting up my arm at the contact. "Let's get out of here." I didn't want him to see the relief in my expression. Eric loved me. And I loved him.

Noah organized the extraction to a tee. We walked out of the hotel without so much as a glance our way and with no malice interception. Once at the vehicles, Eric hugged Sebastian. "Take care of your mother. I'll be back with Alejandro and Pedro," he said, with no doubt in his voice.

Then Layla hugged him, and I squeezed Eric's hand harder than I'd intended because I felt him stiffen. She climbed into the truck with Sebastian behind her.

"Please tell me I didn't just lie," he said, as we watched them make their way in a caravan down the street.

"I can't."

He sighed, and I guided him across the street to my car. "Where are we going?" he asked.

I sighed. "To *my* ex."

And I hoped Finnegan was in a giving mood today.

Chapter Thirty

Eric

"Stop pacing," Zane ordered.

We ended up at the same cabin he'd taken me to after he'd kidnapped me from the club. Not as luxurious as his other properties. This one reminded me of Maine. And I could only take ten paces before I turned back the other way. At this rate, I'd wear out the floor in a few days. It'd been hours since we arrived and hours since Zane attempted to contact Finnegan. The same Finnegan who was a wraith and had been in love with Zane for centuries.

Zane wouldn't tell me anything else, only that Finn had inadvertently shared his soul with Zane, but Zane never loved him, never reciprocated, and Finn hadn't been too happy about it. When I asked Zane what Finn did to him, he closed up. Said nothing. But I knew that was a lie. Like the rest of the lies he'd told me up to date. And to know that I had spilled my guts out in front of everyone, telling him how I really felt. Somehow, knowing the feelings weren't real made them easier to say, and I did feel a whole shitload of relief to get that out of my chest.

Except now Layla thought I was gay. And I hadn't really labeled myself yet. After everything that had happened, my sexuality was the least of my damn worries. I growled and clenched my hands into fists. "What if you're wrong? What if Leander and Alejandro are dead? What if…"

Zane jumped to his feet. "Stop it!"

The tremble in his voice made the windows vibrate. I knew Zane was powerful. Had some sort of strength, but I had yet to see the extent of it. Though the pieces he showed now and again scared the shit out of me, he wouldn't hurt me. Not physically, anyway. "They aren't dead."

"And Pedro?" I asked because I still couldn't believe that Pedro Ortega, Layla's husband who had been near my children for five fucking years, was a malice. "Are you sure?"

"Yes. Leander sensed him and I trust Leander."

I dragged my hand down my face. Leander, the white wolf Sebastian had taken to, was his younger brother. "Why Doofus?" I suddenly asked.

Zane let out a heavy breath, and his body seemed to relax. "Because I told Leander to stop being a Doofus and acting like a mutt. Doofus stuck. I'm surprised you believe me."

I shrugged. "I just saw my son fall out of a terrace on the twentieth floor and disappear. I saw your fangs, and you consumed in flames but not burn. A wolf-man isn't that farfetched."

"You've never asked," Zane said, slowly walking closer to me. Thankfully, he turned into the kitchen to get water.

"What do you mean?"

He looked at me over the cup he was drinking, his throat bobbing as he swallowed. I wondered what he would taste like now. I had the sudden compulsion to lick his throat as he swallowed to feel it against my tongue. He lowered the glass. His eyes darkened, and all my insides jolted to attention. "What are you?" I finally asked.

I felt our combined heartbeats in sync with each other. The feeling surreal. As if we were both on the same frequency. I watched as he approached me until my ass hit the back of the sofa, then he ran a finger from my temple, down my jawline, and cupped my chin so I couldn't look away from him. Not that I would. Zane was gorgeous and strong, and he was *mine.*

"I am of the underworld. I am neither spirit nor corporeal, but both. I am night and day, cycles of the sun and moon. I am interconnected with the world around me. Through sight, sound, and feelings. I feed on emotions. An empath and succubus. But I am not a spell caster. I am not infinite nor immortal and I—" He grabbed my hand and put my palm over his heart. "— I'm in love with you."

I gasped.

"There is no longer denying it. Accept it or not for what it is because one day, it will consume you, and I will be here when you are ready. I do not run from those I care for, nor ignore what fate has given me. I am true to myself, Eric Diaz. Are you?"

I sharply pulled my hand away from his chest, taking a step back to give me much-needed space.

"You were in Maine for me. Why?"

I saw him hesitate briefly.

"I never stopped thinking about you after that night. You've been in my thoughts and heart."

That night in the hotel came heralding through my memories. Aurora's words about how Zane had reacted

227

afterward breached my heart. "And you still let me go. Twice."

"A mistake that won't happen again."

I wanted to believe him. My heart urged me to believe him. There was little choice in the matter. "I thought it'd been a dream, that you hadn't been real. As the years passed by, I thought I'd made it all up."

An expression of unfiltered pain marred his perfect eyes.

I loved this man.

No use denying my feelings for him. No spell to ward them away. Nothing the imagination could heal.

"It is still your choice. Once we get Alejandro back—"

I launched myself at him and slammed my mouth against his to shut him up and just kiss me. I wanted to devour him, consume him, absorb him into my body. He quickly complied and wrapped his arms around me. "I love you, Zane. I love you." My hands were already at his belt, then inside his pants as I felt soft velvet against my palm. I exhaled a sigh of relief as I felt him instantly harden for me and ran my finger along his weeping head.

"I want you inside me, Zane," I said. "I want you to fill me up in every way possible."

Zane bit my bottom lip hard, but not breaking the skin. It forced me to jerk my hips against his thigh. I wanted to be one with him. He spun me around and dropped my pants to my ankles, my ass exposed to him.

"Fuck, Eric, you have a nice ass."

My cheeks heated. A moan later, he slowly dipped his finger along the crease of my ass, then swept down, sliding along my hole. I clenched in response. This was going to hurt, but I didn't care.

"You're a virgin," he said.

I nodded like an idiot. He knew damn well I'd never been with a man.

"I'll make it good for you, Eric. Real good. I promise. But if you want me to stop, just say the word and we don't have to do this. Tell me you understand."

I shook my head, unable to get the words out as his hand started pumping my engorged cock.

"I need to hear you say it, Eric."

"I understand. If I can't take it, I'll tell you to stop."

He turned me around and lifted my shirt over my head, then helped me out of my shoes and pants. Then he stepped away, leaving me confused and cold. His hungry eyes scorched my skin as he slowly took all of me in. I felt about to blow and cupped my shaft, pumping away as I watched how turned on he was. His pupils enlarged; his lips parted. And his smell. That heady scent that was all him grew more powerful, as if he leaked it from his pores. I could've sworn I heard wolves howling in the distance. The place felt infected with an ambient presence that pressed against my exposed, heated skin and I knew it was him.

Zane's aura, his essence, his soul against my body.

"Take me however you want me, Zane."

"This is your first time, Eric. Be careful what you allow me to have."

Allow him to have.

I was in control of him. He was mine to do as I wished. That's what Serena had been trying to tell me. Zane had tethered himself to me. The thought of having him under my control did something inside of me. It made me want to be worthy of it. Of him.

"I am yours tonight, Zane."

That was all it took. He came back at me with a mission. His mouth hungered for mine as I helped him undress. When we were naked, he grabbed my hand and marched me outside. Okay, this hadn't been what I had expected, but the sky was clear, the moon high, and the landscape before us was alive with energy. We walked a few yards to a clearing where the ethereal light of the moonlight beamed down distinctly. Then he released my hand as I watched him step under the light. His light blue eyes had turned blood red as he offered me his hand. "I want everyone to know that you are mine, *chosen*," he said.

A warm trickle of water glazed my skin as I broke through the thin barrier of light to reach him. No, not water, but something else. Something powerful. Under that strange blue light, Zane kissed me. His tongue explored every part of my mouth, leaving nothing unexplored. The desire in us mounted exponentially with every touch. It felt as if we had become one. His desire and mine united. The sensations doubled. I was going to blow my load just by kissing him. Then he led me to the soft ground blanketed in dry leaves and moss. I bit my lip to stop from moaning when he spread my thighs and again seemed to touch every inch of me with his eyes. Then he explored me with his hand, running his finger down my inner thighs to my shaft and then my balls. My body weeping for him.

"Zane, please," I said, though I didn't know what I was pleading for.

I heard him rip a package. Cold, lubed fingers trailed against my hole. I tensed again.

"Relax, Eric."

He licked my shaft from base to tip before drawing me fully into his mouth. I jerked forward, deeper into his mouth, eyes rolling back, enjoying the sensation. He sucked and pulled, and I moaned in euphoric pleasure. He released me with a pop and then kissed me violently. His lips, wet and swollen. The taste of me on his tongue.

"I want you to be loud for me, Eric. Tell me what you want."

"Fuck," I said, lifting my hips again. My legs split apart as his fingers touched my entrance. "I want you, Zane. Fuck. I don't know."

I didn't. I just knew I needed more of him.

"I got you, my chosen. Always."

I nodded like a fool.

"Just relax for me. Can you do that?"

I nodded, and his finger dipped deeper inside me. I felt the immediate burn as he breached my tight hole to his first knuckle. His other hand stroked me tenderly and the two halves of pain and pleasure almost split me in two. As he sank another finger inside of me, I thought I was going to explode. I moaned, loud. The burning, emotional sensation of feeling tore through me.

"Zane," I breathed. "I don't know if I can do this."

"Just a few more seconds. I got you."

He lowered himself and sucked me inside his hot, wet mouth as he continued to pump his finger into my hole until he hit a spot that fired all my nerve endings. "Fuck!" My body lost control. I was taken with his mouth in front and fingers in my ass, hitting my prostate.

"Fuck me, Zane!" I said loud enough to echo into the field. "Now. Please."

I watched as he positioned himself over my entrance, then pushed inside of me. Hunger in his expression sent another burst of heat through me. His pupils were blown, almost all back with a rim of red. The man was so fucking beautiful. Strong arms caged me as I held on to my knees, opening myself wider for him. I loved that he watched himself disappear inside of me. The sense of fullness countered anything else.

"Fuck, Eric. You feel so fucking tight."

No shit. He was inside my ass. My virgin ass! And it was amazing. He started pumping faster, his thrusts deeper until his balls slapped against my ass. I cried out with the same nerve-racking sensations I'd felt when he'd hit my prostate. I'd never had sex like this. *Ever*.

"Touch yourself, Eric. Let me see you come," he said in a rushed breath. I did as he said and started to pump my already weeping cock. Long, tight pulls. The collectedness tantalized my erotic sensation, overwhelming my senses.

It was then I sensed someone watching us, making me hornier. I wanted everyone to know that Zane Crawford was mine. His cock was inside me and his mouth on me.

"I'm coming," I hissed out. My body jerked once, twice, and I exploded between us. Jets of cum squirted on my stomach; my balls clenched along with my ass. One thrust later, Zane let out a guttural, animalistic sound, and he totally consumed me as he spilled his seed inside of me. He continued to jerk, to ride out the euphoria for a few more seconds before he finally slumped on top of me, using his forearms to keep from squashing me.

Zane gave me a heated kiss that left my lips swelled. Both of us sated to the max. Tired. I could've fallen asleep here against the dead leaves. "I love you, Eric."

Those words pushed all doubts away. They were real. "I love you, Zane."

As we lay together, Finn walked out of the tree line, and I hated the way he gave Zane a slow once over. Jealousy curled around my belly because I knew they had probably fucked. Probably the same way Zane and I had just fucked.

Zane must've sensed something because he growled and then kissed me deeply, claiming me all over again. When he finished, Finnegan was gone.

"We need him," I said.

"Unfortunately, yes." Zane climbed to his feet and helped me up.

I winced as my ass clenched up and his fluids dripped down the back of my thighs, down my legs. With the endorphins gone, I felt every onslaught I'd allowed to happen to my body. And it felt good.

Zane took my hand and we walked back to the cabin. I plucked my clothes from the floor and started for the bathroom, where I dressed quickly while Zane disappeared into the bedroom. I met Finn in the living room. The man speared me with his black eyes.

"Will you still love him if he cannot save your son?" Finnegan asked.

"Yes," I said. "I will always love him."

Finn sighed and got to his feet. "Then you're going to have to do exactly as I say."

I narrowed my eyes at the wraith, realizing one

thing: he and I wanted to keep Zane safe. I had to believe that included bringing back Leander and Alejandro, so I listened.

And prayed for the first time in five years.

Chapter Thirty-One

Zane

Eric walked into the bedroom with a glass of amber liquid. I dressed quickly, then took the drink from his hand and gulped it down.

"Do you trust Finn?" Eric asked. He took back the glass.

"In this. Yes. He won't do anything to hurt me, and losing you would hurt me."

"I don't know what or who to trust anymore."

I cupped his face, and whether he realized it or not, he leaned into my touch as if seeking more of me. "We are bound. It means we have joined our souls. We are one."

He lifted his bloodshot eyes to mine.

I felt everything in those brown eyes.

"Together, we can get through this. No matter what information Finn gives us. *Together.*"

Without a word, he nodded.

I gently kissed his lips before we headed downstairs to meet Finn, but it wasn't Finn. The man sitting on the armchair had hair as black as midnight, and black eyes to match. His skin was pale, as if it had no life running through him. Wearing a silk black button-down shirt and black slacks, he wasn't handsome or ugly. He was someone you'd forget as soon as he left your presence. A shadow lurking in the darkness. His presence stirred malice in the air.

Eric felt it too. He didn't move closer to the man.

"Lucifer," I greeted. I kept my voice neutral, my expression schooled, to show nothing.

Slowly, his eyes met mine. It felt like a thousand spiders crawled along my flesh, digging their tiny legs into my skin. I fought to keep from screaming. "Zane," he said, then dragged his eyes to Eric beside me. "And your *chosen*." He motioned to the empty sofa in front of him. "Please, sit."

I held Eric's hand and we both sat.

"Congratulations are in order. Finn has been raging about your binding. Excellent choice." The smile on Lucifer's face would send any man to madness. Eric trembled beside me, and I absorbed his fear.

"Thank you," I said, keeping my voice even. "I hadn't expected you."

"Of course not. You expected my son. The one you tainted. I'm afraid I sent him on an errand."

Ever since Finn had shown interest in me for something other than torture, Lucifer had blamed me. As if I could control anyone's emotions. "Why are you here?"

Lucifer tapped the arm of the chair with long, deft fingers. "I hear you've lost something in my realm. I'm here as a courtesy to you. I assume you want them back."

"Yes, we do."

Lucifer licked his pale lips, his eyes taking in every inch of both Eric and me, measuring, calculating. I'd seen that look before. "What are you willing to give me for it?"

And there it was. The real reason he was here. He wanted something. I had to be careful in bartering with Lucifer. Lies and deception coated his tongue. I hoped Eric would keep his mouth shut. "I'm assuming you have something in mind?"

The gleam in his eyes sent shivers coursing through me. "You know what I want. What I've wanted since I tasted you, son of wrath."

"Me," I said dryly. "You want me."

"Yes. Say the word. You return to Hell with me and the human and the shifter go free. Just like that."

I opened my mouth to say yes when Eric spoke.

"No," he said.

Lucifer's smile faded as he turned his attention to Eric.

"No. You will not take Zane from me."

"You are willing to subject your son to torture, to pain, to sorrows for a good fuck?"

Eric swallowed. "Show me."

"Excuse me?"

"Show me my son. Prove that you have them both."

Lucifer's face turned dangerous. I wanted to tell Eric to shut up. Not to piss off the Prince of Hell.

"You can't, can you. Because you don't have them. They're not *in* Hell."

Lucifer pinched a nonexistent lint off his pants and flicked it into the air. "Not yet. But it's only a matter of time."

Eric slowly got to his feet. "Get out. You have no power over the Anunnaki."

Lucifer didn't move. He turned his raging fire eyes on me. "You will pay for this."

Then he popped out of existence as though never here. Eric turned to me, his eyes two golden flames. I felt the sofa under me begin to swallow me into its depth. I tried to stand but couldn't. "Eric." My voice barely audible.

Eric looked at me. "I'm sorry. I have to do this alone."

The liquor he'd given me tasted like acid on my tongue. He'd drugged me. I reached out to grab him, to make him stay, but my arm floated in front of me with no strength.

Time meant nothing in the world of dreams.

It paced slow or fast with no limitations. In my dreams, I'd grown old. In my dreams, I had faced my fears. I'd lived a human life. I lived a life with a child and Serena. In my dreams, I married Eric.

But life was not made up of dreams. One couldn't live in the dream world.

Reality had to sift through.

I clawed my way into the reality in which I knew Eric faced Lucifer. Where he quite possibly faced the malice, the darkness. The aether was a potent place full of temptations. For power, lust, anything a man could want. None of it real.

I tried to claw my way to the surface.

Eric!

I felt him nearby. His solid presence just beyond the darkness.

Eric!

I breached the surface and felt the cool breeze on my hand, my face, then my body as I took a deep breath.

I opened my eyes and blinked away the haze until

my vision cleared and I saw my mother. I couldn't speak.

"Calm down, Zane. He's fine."

I hadn't realized I was growling until I sat up. I searched the faces around me and didn't see Eric.

"He's in the bedroom."

I swung my legs over the sofa and got to my feet. "Leander?"

"He's in the bedroom too, but Pedro is missing."

I headed that way and entered the bedroom. Leander's wolf whimpered and raised his head. Sprawled on the bed next to Alejandro. Eric held a towel to his son's forehead, tears smothering his ash-covered face.

"He's alive. He just won't wake up," Eric said.

Cuts and scratches marred his hands and his face. I wanted to yell, to demand he never, *ever* leave me behind again. I said nothing. Instead, I stood next to him and took his hand in mine. He turned to me and wrapped his arms around my waist, his head on my chest as I caressed him. "Your mother says he's safer here than at a hospital, but he won't wake up."

I turned to look at Leander watching us. The wolf version of him was stronger, the reason Leander preferred that shape. I could only imagine what happened the few hours they'd been in the aether. Time worked differently in the other realms. Even if it wasn't Hell, it was nothing good.

"Baby, he will. The important thing is that you got him out." I cupped Eric's face and forced him to look at me. "And don't ever, *ever*, fucking do that again." I kissed him, full on the mouth, possessively. Eric gave me everything back. I tasted his tears on my tongue.

"He's strong. I feel it. Just like his father."

Not a lie. I felt the kid's strength. I also felt something different in the kid. A second presence I didn't want to mention. I glared at Leander, who dug his head into Alejandro's side as if daring me to move him.

"I'm going to make preparations to take him to the mansion. We can protect him better there."

Eric nodded and trusted that I at least could get us home.

Epilogue

Finnegan

Two weeks later...

Their lovemaking was slow and passionate. The scent of musk and sex was heavy in the air. A union, a binding, between two souls. Something the wraith would never have. His father had forbidden it. Had punished him for loving the Anunnaki prophesied to destroy him. Lucifer had bound his soul to Zane so that Finnegan would always remember the consequences of going against his father.

A lesson he hadn't learned.

"I should smite you where you stand," Lucifer hissed beside him.

The two on the bed, too entranced in each other to sense their presence, continued their writhing and moaning of desire. "Do it, then." *Put me out of this misery.*

Zane slid kisses along Eric's jaw, reaching his lips. "I love you, Eric," he said as his hips jerked into the other man's erection. Their heated, sweaty bodies fused as one. Tongues warred for control, and hands touched where mouths followed.

"I love you, Zane. You are *mine*," Eric said back.

A painful need flowed through Finn's body. A need that would never find release. A need that fueled

241

his insanity. Death would've been kinder. But his father was a sadistic bastard.

Finn had devised the plan to break the shifter and the human from the aether without Lucifer's knowledge. Finnegan had told Eric of Lucifer's plan to lie to get Zane into Hell. It had been Finn who carried the human out before Lucifer found him. His only ask was for Eric to promise to keep Zane safe. To keep Zane out of Hell. The only solace the wraith enjoyed was Zane, even if the immortal could not love him in return. Finnegan's sleep potion had worked almost too well. It took Zane hours to wake up. By that time, his family had arrived, and Finn had escaped unnoticed. In shadow.

"I prefer to see you suffer," his father said.

Finnegan sighed.

"Just remember, there is more I can do to make you suffer. Do not forget it, son of my blood." Lucifer popped out of existence.

Lucifer, however, was wrong. He'd erred in casting the ultimate torture unto the wraith. There was nothing more he could do that would hurt worse than the hollowness inside Finn's chest. The aching pain of watching his love with another, knowing he would never have Zane. Never be sated and experience his own release.

Even death would be a reprieve.

The wraith floated out of existence and reappeared inside the boy's room. The shifter finally left him alone. The boy with the golden locks and green-colored eyes. The boy who had sacrificed himself to save another.

A strength not born out of love, but duty. A guardian's duty.

Finnegan placed his hand on the kid's forehead. The contact sent a jolt of power flowing between them. The aether had awoken something inside the human boy. A once dormant power lifted. Soon, the boy would awaken already ascended.

A Protector of blood. The eldest son.

"An enemy of thy enemy with a destiny to fulfill."

Death awaits.

A word about the author...

Elle Arroyo grew up in Chicago where she writes paranormal romance.

Before she started writing, Elle got her undergraduate degree in Psychology with a minor in Criminal Justice. She then went on to work in foster care programs, mental health facilities, and youth organizations within the Latinx Community.

When not writing, Elle spends time with her family, binge watches anime, and reads anything with romance in it.

Elle continues to live in Chicago with her family.
https://ellearroyo.wordpress.com/